TWIST IN THE TALE

SHORT STORIES

VOLUME 1

A J BOOTHMAN

SECOND EDITION

ALVASDA KEREZARD

TWIST IN THE TALE SHORT STORIES

Published by Alvasda Kerezard 2023

ISBN 978-1-916537-06-4

First published 2021.

CONTENTS

TWIST IN THE TALE SHORT STORIES

THE ATTIC

TWIST IN THE TALE SHORT STORIES

"Still no news of Lucy Robbins, the student who went missing last week."

The small, squat man turned off the radio and knelt on the floor. He struggled as he rolled the old rug, his thick glasses steaming up as he breathed heavily. Despite being over six feet long, pushing and straining he managed to flip it over and over until it was a rather bulky log. The kitchen floor was a mess, it would have to wait for now. He slipped a length of rope under each end and tied it securely. Gripping one end firmly he dragged it across the floor. The heavy weight made progress difficult as he staggered into the hall. He let it go and wiped his brow, looking up the daunting stairs. Kneeling down he pushed the log up causing it to bend slightly in the middle. He heaved it against the wall and pushed it up until it was almost vertical. Placing his arms around the middle and using the wall for support he lifted it onto his shoulder Positioning it as comfortably as he could he made his way slowly up the stairs. He panted continually, moving gradually, one careful step at a time. On the landing he put the rug down and reached up to the cord hanging from the hatch leading into the attic. He gripped it firmly and pulled it down forcibly. The ladder protruded from the hole, he took the bottom rung and extended it to the ground. Wiping his glasses he stared apprehensively at the rug, then the ladder, then the small opening. He put his glasses back on and shunted the log forward, resting it against the rungs. Bending his knees he gripped the bottom and began sliding it up the inclined ladder. It inched its way up until the top entered the gap. He rested the rug on his bent knee as he adjusted his grip and regained his breath. Once more the log ascended until the bottom was on his chest. He got his hands underneath and with one mighty shove and groan he drove his hands above his head. The rug toppled onto the wooden floorboards with a thud. He clambered up, turning on the light as he entered. The naked bulb flickered into life providing a dim light. The small space was crammed with boxes of junk. He moved a few to create a space along one side, dragged the rug into it and pushed it against the wall. Then he replaced the boxes so it was hidden from view. He turned off the light and descended.

Back in the kitchen he went to the sink and filled a bucket with hot wate pouring in a liberal amount of detergent. He peeled rubber gloves over his hands and knelt on the floor, dipping his brush into the bucket and scrubbing the lino vigorously.

An hour later he scrutinised the kitchen. Everything was in its proper place, crockery in the cupboard, pots on their frame and the knives neatly in their wooden block. He felt exhausted and traipsed up the stairs to bed oblivious to the fly on the hatch.

Early the following morning he sat in the kitchen, fully dressed, eating breakfast and feeling refreshed after a good night's sleep. He heard the metallic clink of the letterbox closing and ambled out into the hall. The newspaper was lying on the carpet. He picked it up and read the front-page headline as he walked back to the kitchen.

HAVE YOU SEEN LUCY ROBBINS?

Sitting at the table he spread the newspaper out and read while he spooned the cereal into his mouth. Below the headline there was a photo of the missing girl. Her auburn hair cascaded around her young, innocent face as she smiled for the camera. The police were no closer to finding her and were requesting any information from the public that would help. Finishing the bowl he got up and went to the sink. He turned on the tap and ran the water, placing his hand under the stream until it went from lukewarm to hot. Placing the plug securely he squirted the washing up liquid into the steaming water and put on his rubber gloves. He placed the bowl and spoon in the water, cleaning them thoroughly with the brush. The items were dried quickly and put back in their places before pulling the plug in the sink. He wiped down the table top with a clean cloth before picking up the newspaper and ascending the stairs.

As he reached the landing a fly buzzed past his face causing him to instinctively sweep his hand through the air. He watched as it landed high up on the wall. Carefully and silently he rolled up the newspaper. He moved stealthily towards the fly, tightening his grip as he raised the paper high over his head. For a moment he paused behind the stationary fly. With one swift movement he struck the wall with a thud. He looked in disgust at the red and black mark vivid on the white wallpaper. Putting the paper down he went into the bathroom and came back with a wet cloth. He delicately dabbed the mark until it was gone. Glancing down at the unravelled newspaper the remains of the fly were splattered across the face of the missing girl.

It was getting dark when he returned home, the winter making daylight shorter and shorter. He went upstairs and turned the landing light on. A fly buzzed past his head and landed on the hatch beside two other flies. On the wall below was another fly. He descended the stairs and back out through the front door.

The radio was playing in the local shop.

"There is still no trace of missing student, Lucy Robbins."

"It's terrible," commented the old woman behind the counter.

He remained silent and looked at her.

"That young girl," she elaborated. "The one that's missing."

"Oh, yes," he mumbled.

"Probably dead. When they go missing for so long they usually turn up dead. So many bad people in the world."

He stayed quiet and thought about the missing girl.

"What would you like?"

She must have been about nineteen.

"Hello?"

He became aware of the woman looking enquiringly at him.

"Fly spray. Fly spray, please."

"Generally don't get flies once the weather gets colder," she observed reaching up to the shelf behind and removing a can with a picture of a fly emblazoned on the side. "Anything else today?"

"No."

"That's £2.99 then".

He removed a small money purse from his pocket and fumbled with the coins as the news continued on the radio.

"Lucy Robbins went missing from her home last week."

"It's that rug."

He looked up startled dropping the purse causing coins to spill out onto the floor. Kneeling down he scrambled frantically to retrieve the money.

"That old rug, attracting the flies," continued the old woman leaning over the counter and watching him.

"Oh, yes, I suppose so," he gabbled quietly.

"You should throw it out."

"No," he said abruptly standing up.

She was visibly taken aback.

"I mean, it will be worth a lot of money one day," he added hastily.

He counted the coins out on the counter, grabbed the can and hurried away.

Back at home he went immediately up to the landing. Several flies were stationary on the hatch and top of the wall. He shook the can vigorously and removed the lid. The spray filled the air as he targeted each fly in turn watching as they fell lifeless to the ground. The atmosphere was heavy with pesticide. He went downstairs and returned with a small handheld vacuum. He sucked the dead flies from the carpet, ensuring he got each one, smiling with satisfaction as he surveyed the spotless area.

The following morning he was up early. He went out onto the landing and was horrified to see the hatch covered in flies. Rushing downstairs he got the can and held it high over his head, spraying everywhere until the smell of pesticide was pervasive. He quickly vacuumed up the mound of dead flies. Standing back he looked up pensively. He pulled the cord, extended the ladder and climbed up, can in hand. Even before he turned on the light he could hear the sporadic buzzing. As the attic illuminated he could see the insects flitting through the air. They were denser behind the boxes. He moved them to one side and looked in horror at the rug covered with flies, like a black netting. Feverishly, he sprayed up and down, his finger locked on the button until the nozzle spluttered and ran dry. A thick, suffocating cloud filled the air. He covered his mouth as he gasped and coughed, retreating to the ladder and descending quickly. Putting on his overcoat hurriedly, he opened the front door, causing the newspaper on the floor to be crushed against the wall. As it slammed shut the newspaper unravelled exposing the front-page headline.

POLICE INTENSIFY SEARCH
FOR LUCY ROBBINS

Inside the local shop he placed a tube of black bin liners and roll of masking tape on the counter. The old woman looked up from the open newspaper.

"Still no sign of that young girl," she said pressing the keys on the till. He remained silent glancing at the upside-down article.

"I think it's terrible, far too many weirdos out there," she continued. "Do you want a bag for these?"

"No, I can put them in my coat," he replied putting the tape in one side pocket and the bin liners in the other.

"It's terrible a young woman cannot even walk safely down the street now," she continued returning to the newspaper.

"Mmmm," he mumbled, walking quickly across the store and opening the door.

"Did you do it?."

He stopped dead and turned to look at her with a startled expression on his face.

"Get rid of the flies?"

"Oh, yes," he muttered before disappearing into the street.

He went into the kitchen and took a pair of scissors from the drawer. As he ascended the stairs he could smell the pesticide. On the landing he scanned the walls and ceiling. Everything was clear. He pulled down the ladder and entered the attic. There was a powerful smell of pesticide and a faint cloud hung in the air. He removed a handkerchief, folded it into a triangle and tied it around his head covering his nose and mouth. Dead flies covered the floorboards. He knelt down in front of the rug and began to work a bin liner over one end. By lifting the heavy rug slightly he was able to affix the bag and sidle it down each side until it was fully extended. He then moved to the opposite end and slid a bag over until the two bags overlapped in the middle. It was hard work, he wiped the perspiration from his brow with the back of his hand. He cut a strip of masking tape from the role and stuck it to the top bin liner, then another and another, working it along the open edge until he had a strong seal. The process was then repeated to add a second layer of bin liners. He stood up and admired his work.

The following day he woke up early as usual and got dressed. On the landing there was still a faint trace of pesticide but no flies anywhere to be seen. He allowed himself a smile as he jaunted downstairs. The newspaper was lying on the floor behind the front door. Early this morning, he thought, picking it up and walking into the kitchen. He removed a bowl from the cupboard, filled it with cereal and covered it in milk. Sitting at the table he read the front-page headline.

FEARS MOUNT FOR LUCY ROBBINS

They would never find her now he decided.

It was dark when he returned. He opened the door and immediately heard the sound of faint buzzing above. Quickly he closed it and went to the foot of the stairs. The buzzing was getting louder causing him to gaze up anxiously into the darkness. He moved his hand slowly towards the light switch. Pausing as the din above grew louder, he pressed the switch down and illuminated the landing. The wall was covered with a curtain of flies as others swarmed in all directions through the still air. He turned and hurried back out through the door.

The old woman was behind the counter stooped over the open newspaper while at the back of the store a stocky man wearing a baseball cap was browsing through the magazines on the shelves.

"Back again?" she enquired looking up.

"Yes," he replied apprehensively, approaching the counter.

He looked down at the open paper and the smiling face of Lucy Robbins.

"They still haven't found her," observed the old woman.

"No."

"Probably dead, poor thing. Murdered by some mad man."

He stayed silent, staring at the photo.

"What are you after today?"

"Oh, umm, fly spray, I need some more fly spray. Something stronger."

"Do you still have a fly problem? You know, that's strange at this time of year," she pondered looking at the rows of cannisters and containers behind her.

15

She took down a red plastic bottle labelled "Strong Insecticide" above the black symbol of a skull and cross bones.

"This is the strongest thing I have," she said placing it on the counter.

He studied the sinister bottle.

"Do you have a pump?"

"A pump?"

"You need to pour it into a hand pump to spray it."

He looked concerned.

"I have one here somewhere" she said crouching down and ferreting around below the counter.

She stood up and placed a small hand pump on the counter.

"There you are. Anything else?"

"No," he replied, hurriedly taking out his purse.

"That's £40".

He looked up, momentarily surprised at the price before removing four crisp £10 notes.

"Be careful using that," said a gruff voice behind.

He turned to see the face of the man in the baseball cap standing holding a couple of magazines and a tabloid newspaper.

"That's strong stuff. What is it? Ants? Bugs?

"Flies," he replied quietly, hastily gathering up his things.

16

"Flies?," he questioned incredulously. "At this time of year?"

He nodded.

"Can't be flies" Do you want me to take a look? I run a small pest extermination business."

"No," he blurted hurriedly. "I can manage."

"My van's outside, I can take a quick look now if you like.

"I'm fine, thanks all the same," he said rushing across the store and disappearing into the street.

In the kitchen he carefully poured the pesticide into the pump. He walked up the stairs gradually with one hand under the pump and the other gripping the handle firmly, with his finger on the trigger. At the top he squeezed the trigger and fired. The pump hissed as the spray covered the wall. Flies plummeted to the ground as he swept the nozzle through the air. The atmosphere was thick with the smell of the pesticide. He stopped and tied his handkerchief over his nose and mouth as he looked at the dead flies covering the carpet. Yanking the cord he opened the hatch and lowered the ladders. The buzzing was incessant. He gripped the pump tight and ascended cautiously, one rung at a time. The hum grew louder and louder. At the top he turned on the light and looked in horror at the swarming flies. He fired in all directions, filling the attic with a thick cloud, so thick he began to splutter and his eyes watered. Scrambling to get out he descended quickly, coughing as he did. He pushed the ladder up and closed the hatch with a bang. Pulling the handkerchief from his mouth he spluttered violently and wiped his eyes. As he recovered he remained still and listened. Above all was quiet. He breathed a huge sigh of relief. Suddenly, he was startled by a loud knocking. The blood froze in his veins. Someone was at the front door. Again he heard the knocking as he made his way slowly down the stairs. He opened the door slightly and poked his head around, it was the pest controller from the store.

"I hope you don't mind but the woman in the shop gave me your address."

"How does she know my address?," he asked suspiciously.

"From your newspaper delivery."

He had forgotten his paper delivery.

"I wanted to check up on your fly infestation. It's rare to get it at this time of year."

"It's all fine. They've gone."

"Already? I'd better check for any eggs," said the pest controller stepping forward.

"NO!" he replied panicked.

"If you don't get all the eggs the flies will return."

"I checked thoroughly. I have to go now," he said closing and locking the door.

The pest controller shook his head and shrugged as he walked back to his van. He got in looking down at the headline on the front page of the tabloid on the seat beside him.

WHERE IS LUCY ROBBINS?

He glanced up at the house, strange guy, he thought, before starting the engine and driving away.

Inside the house the only sound was the vacuum cleaner coming from the landing. He swept it back and forth until not a dead fly was to be seen. Back in the kitchen he made a hearty dinner, watched a bit of television and went to bed at his usual early time. He lay in bed listening to the silence and smiled. As he drifted off all was as it should be.

He was woken by a light buzzing coming from above. Opening his eyes he squinted into the darkness. His clock displayed 4am. The humming above was incessant. He ambled up groggily, putting on his dressing gown and slippers. Opening the bedroom door the humming got louder. He looked up at the attic, no flies but there was a constant hum coming from it. Tentatively he pulled the cord. As the hatch opened the buzzing became louder. He peered through the opening, there was quite a racket but nothing was to be seen. Lowering the ladders he climbed up apprehensively. Inside the noise was deafening, sound was coming from all directions. He switched on the light. The air was thick with flies, every wall was matted in a black curtain of the insects. He looked in horror at the rug covered in eggs. Suddenly the flies started buzzing around his head. He swatted his hands wildly through the air catching the bulb and casting the attic into darkness. So many flies, he could feel them all over his body, his neck, his face, his bare feet. He tried to sweep them away but they kept coming in relentless waves. There seemed to be no escape from his invisible enemies. As he felt them crawling under his pyjamas he became hysterical, spinning out of control, tugging frenziedly at his clothes. He staggered back frantically, tripping and falling back through the open hatch, landing heavily in a crumpled heap on the floor below.

The low winter sun streamed through the windows illuminating the inside of the house. On the landing the lifeless body lay covered in flies. The letterbox snapped and the newspaper rustled to the ground. The bright rays shone on the front-page headline: *Lucy Robbins found alive and well.*

SHEEBA

TWIST IN THE TALE SHORT STORIES

The man crept through the deserted yard, each step slow and deliberate in the darkness, any noise might alert the security guard. He could see him through the window of his small hut, the lamp inside illuminating his slumbering figure slumped over the desk. The changing images from the television screen in front of him flickered on his balding head. The man stood still and listened to the faint sound of voices and sporadic audience laughter. He moved stealthily away from the hut towards the warehouse. The night air was cold and dry, he pulled the balaclava down over his mouth and tucked it into the collar of his coat ensuring that no part of his neck was exposed to the icy breeze. He walked quietly along the side of the building, past the metal shutters over the warehouse entrance, past the windows covered with iron grills, to a small side door. He stopped and studied the door running his hand over the single yale lock. A chain is only as strong as its weakest link, he thought as he removed a leather case from his coat pocket and knelt down. He placed it on the ground, carefully unzipping it and opening the flaps. The small tools were arranged neatly in a row, all different shapes and sizes. He placed the tip of his finger onto the lock and felt the grooves before selecting a tension tool from the case and inserting it into the bottom of the lock. Reaching back down to the case he took out a lock pick. It was delicate work but he had perfected it over the years into a fine art, taking a great deal of pride in his work. He made the tension tool taut with his left hand while he meticulously probed the cylinder with the lock pick in his right. It was lamentable that the young men in his profession lacked these skills, choosing instead to clumsily smash a window. They gave him a bad name. He could feel the barrels turning in the cylinder. The lock clicked. He returned the tools precisely to their correct places, zipped up the case and put it back in his pocket. These instruments were like trusted, old friends to him. He opened the door cautiously and entered. Once the door was closed he turned on a small torch. What would he find today? He shone the beam onto the shelves. Rows upon rows of boxes with the contents scrawled on the cardboard with a black marker. He walked slowly down the aisle scrutinising each: dolls, glasses, laptops, an eclectic mix he noted. Laptops would generate good money but too bulky to carry. He continued: curtains, toasters, mobile phones; that was better. Carefully he reached up taking the box from the shelf and placing it on the floor. He opened the lid. Phones were scattered in a haphazard fashion. He picked one up and examined it, top of the range with the protective seal still covering the screen. Quickly he produced a small canvas bag from inside his coat and scooped the phones inside until it was full. He closed the box and replaced it on the shelf. Switching off the torch he moved quickly down the aisle. He opened the door quietly, remaining still and listening. All was reassuringly silent. He stepped through the door and closed it behind him before disappearing into the night.

The cool morning breeze rustled through the branches of the trees and the sun rose in the clear blue sky shining brightly on the warehouse. Inside a small man in a donkey jacket lifted the box labelled "phones" from the shelf, placed it on the floor and opened the lid.

"Aaaargh! What the hell do I pay that security guard for?" exclaimed a portly man in a tweed jacket and open collared shirt pacing up and down the aisle.

He ran his hands through his hair in an agitated fashion, his raging eyes looking at the half empty contents.

"Probably asleep or watching porn on that damn telly!" he continued.

The small man in the donkey jacket bowed his head. A skinny man ambled towards them, a grin spreading across his thin, rat-like face.

"Hmmm, phones this time," he mused kneeling down and examining the box. "Top brands too. Where d'ya get these? Fell off the back of a lorry or flew out of a factory window?

"Never mind where I got them, that's the second robbery this month! I'm gonna fire that useless guy, put one of these dolls in charge," he continued to rant pulling a doll out from a nearby box and holding it up by the leg. "What I can't understand is how he is getting in, Jack. No windows are smashed, no doors broken down."

"Probably picking locks," speculated Jack standing up. "I noticed some scratches on the side door."

"Picking locks? Who's robbing me, Raffles?"

"This guy is good, very professional. He sneaks in, takes what he wants and leaves."

"Oh great, perhaps I can get him a good work award. Do you find this funny, Larry?"

"No boss," muttered the man in the donkey jacket, lowering his head again and staring at the ground.

"What I want to know is how can I stop him, or better still catch him and give him a good hiding?"

"Relax, Doug, what you need is a big dog," said Jack.

"That's gonna cost me."

"Nah, I'll do you a good price, just leave it to me."

The sun sunk lower in the sky, the shadows creeping slowly across the lawn. The little girl shivered and moved onto the last remaining patch of grass not in the shade. She twirled her pig tail around her finger and picked up the small ball, throwing it towards the swing. A large dog raced across the garden swiftly pouncing on it. She smiled with delight as it trotted back with the ball in its mouth, its brown almond eyes sparkling and its pointed ears pricked. The dog dropped the ball from its jagged teeth at her feet. She knelt down and put her arms around the dog's neck hugging it tight and rocking back and forth. The dog's tail wagged and its pink tongue licked her face making her giggle.

"That tickles," she gushed scrunching up her face as the wet tongue lapped her cheek. "I love you Sheeba."

She stroked the dog, her small, soft hand gliding gently from its golden head and down the black fur on its back.

A white van pulled up across the street. Inside a skinny man started rolling a cigarette. He placed it between his thin lips and struck a match, the flame illuminating his rat-like face.

"That's the dog, there, Larry"

"It looks far too tame, Jack" replied his accomplice in the donkey jacket. "Look how it plays with that girl."

"It can be trained, it's an Alsatian, isn't it. Just look at those sharp teeth. Hold on, someone's coming."

A tall man in a trilby opened the gate and entered the garden. The dog broke free and sped across the lawn towards him. It rose on its sturdy hind legs and placed its paws on his chest causing him to stagger back as the force knocked off his hat.

"One of these days you're going to knock me over, Sheeba," he said patting the dog firmly as it licked his face.

"Daddy!" shouted the little girl running and hugging his legs.

He put his hand on her head and ruffled her hair as he struggled to maintain his balance.

"Alright, alright, " he chuckled as Sheeba dropped to the ground..

"Almost time for dinner, Maddie."

"Just a little while longer," she pleaded looking up with her big blue eyes.

"I'll call you when its ready."

She released his legs and ran towards the ball followed by Sheeba, picking it up and throwing it again. Her father watched and smiled as he walked towards the house and disappeared inside.

"Now, Jack?"

"Not yet, we'll wait until the little girl goes in. Have you got the meat?"

Larry unwrapped the package on his lap.

"Steak! And look at the size of it! How much did that cost?"

"£15".

"£15! I told you to get a cheap cut."

"Look, it's a big dog, we need a big piece of meat, don't we."

"That's coming out of your £100."

They watched as the little girl climbed on to the dog's broad back and rode it around the garden. Jack removed a container from the glove compartment and unscrewed the lid.

"Hold it out."

Jack held the container up and sprinkled white powder on top of the steak then rubbed it in.

"MADDIE! DINNER TIME!"

Her father stood in the doorway. She dismounted, gave Sheeba a hug and skipped towards the house. The door closed and the dog lay down on the lawn with its head up and its eyes alert. Inside the van Jack looked along the deserted street. He checked the side mirrors, all was quiet and still as the sun disappeared below the horizon.

"Right let's go," he said taking the meat and opening the door.

Despite crossing the road as inconspicuously as they could Sheeba was immediately alerted to their presence. Her sharp penetrating eyes never faltered from them, analysing their every move. They stopped before the gate. The dog stood up.

"I'm not going in there with that," whispered Larry fearfully.

"Don't worry, we won't need to."

Sheeba moved slowly and deliberately towards them, each paw landing assuredly, exuding latent power.

"Maybe this isn't such a good idea," murmured Larry backing away as the dog got closer.

Jack removed the meat from the packing and threw it into the garden. Sheeba approached it cautiously, lowering her nose and sniffing it. She looked up at the men watching on anxiously.

"It's not falling for it, let's go, Jack."

Sheeba sniffed the meat again and then gobbled it hungrily, her sharp teeth tearing it to shreds until nothing was left. The men observed silently. Sheeba approached the gate and stuck her snout through the slit.

"What now, Jack?"

"Just wait."

The dog slumped onto its side and lay still.

"Is it dead?"

"Nah, just knocked out," replied Jack opening the gate. "You get the back legs."

The two men picked up the sleeping dog.

"Christ it's heavy," panted Larry struggling across the street.

They opened the back of the van and placed the dog inside. A minute later the van was gone and the garden empty.

Dark clouds covered the sky and a cold morning chill cut through the air. The back door opened.

"Sheeba!"

"Zip up your coat, Maddie!", called her father from the kitchen as she skipped across the dew-covered grass.

"Sheeba! Where are you?"

She knelt in front on the wooden kennel and peeked inside. An empty basket lay on the floor. She stood up and looked around with a mixture of worry and bewilderment. Where was Sheeba? She ran back into the house standing in the kitchen with her bottom lip trembling

"Daddy, Sheeba has gone."

He moved swiftly into the garden scanning all around.

"SHEEBA! SHEEBA!"

He opened the gate and ran along the deserted street, his mind racing. This was unlike the dog to wander off. He reached the main road, cars and lorries roared by in both directions. Slowly he meandered back, what was he going to tell Maddie?

"Where is Sheeba, Daddy?"

"She'll be back soon, " he replied reassuringly as her mother watched from the doorway

"Has she run away?"

Her pretty eyes began to well with tears. He put his arms around her.

"No, she's just gone for a little walk."

"But she goes for a walk with me."

Rain drops began to fall on the window.

"Go and play with your dollies and I'll go and find Sheeba."

Maddie trudged from the kitchen with her head bowed. Her father and mother watched as she climbed the stairs to her bedroom.

"I'll make some signs and put them on the lampposts," he said picking up his phone and looking at the pictures.

He stopped at a photo of Maddie sitting on the grass, smiling radiantly with her arms cuddling Sheeba. Her mother looked over his shoulder.

"What will you do if you can't find her?"

"I have to find her."

Sheeba sauntered around the derelict barn, sniffing the ground.

"Good size dog," observed the old man removing the pipe from his mouth.

"Can you train it?" enquired Jack eagerly.

"Of course. Smart dogs, Alsatians."

"How long?"

"About two weeks."

"And £200 as we agreed on the phone."

The old man sucked on his pipe and nodded.

Maddie's dad walked down the street, every lamppost displaying the same sign: "HAVE YOU SEEN THIS DOG?" emblazoned in big, black letters across the top and a photo of Sheeba below bounding across the grass towards the camera. Her eyes sparkling and her golden fur glowing in the sun. It had been over two weeks since her disappearance. As he approached the house he could see Maddie in her customary position at the gate waiting. Her face saddened again as she could see her father returning alone once more.

"When is Sheeba coming home, Daddy?"

"Soon, Maddie, soon," he said soothingly as he picked her up and carried her into the house.

"Wash your hands for dinner, Maddie," instructed her mother.

They watched as she walked dejectedly into the bathroom.

"Maybe we should just get another dog," she suggested.

"I'm going out again tonight."

Larry stood outside the warehouse covered from head to foot in padding, wire mesh covering his face and a stick dangling loosely from his hand. Jack stood a short distance away with Sheeba on a lead.

"Are you sure this is safe, Jack?"

"Perfectly safe, you're well protected."

Doug came out of the office.

"Is this the dog?"

"Yep, just collected it from the trainer."

"Doesn't look very ferocious," said Doug sceptically scrutinising the dog sitting patiently with its tongue hanging out.

"Just wait and see," replied Jack unclipping the lead and stepping back.

"Raise the stick in a threatening manner, Larry!"

Larry lifted the stick tentatively above his head. Sheeba watched him with curiosity, remaining seated.

"Wave it about a bit!"

Larry waved it unenthusiastically in the air. Sheeba remained motionless.

"I'm going back in," said Doug testily.

"No, wait. Larry shout and be more violent with the stick!

"ROOAARR!

Larry let out a huge scream and shook the stick aggressively. Sheeba raced across the yard and launched herself at Larry, her strong paws landing on his chest and knocking him to the hard ground.

"ARRRGH!"

The sharp teeth tore at the wire mesh covering his face.

"That's more like it, Jack" praised Doug. "I thought they usually grab the arm."

"That's police dogs, this one has been trained to kill. Did you see how it went for the face and attacked without barking, it's like a ninja."

"How much?"

"£800"

"£800!"

"Well its'£400 for the trainer and £200 each for me and Larry," lied Jack.

Doug looked at the dog viciously mauling the helpless figure thrashing around on the ground.

"Jack! Get it off me!"

"Heel!"

Sheeba let go of the mesh and trotted back.

"Ok. £800 it is."

"I'll put some "Beware of the dog" signs up."

Doug observed a dazed Larry as he staggered to his feet, parts of the padding and mesh ripped.

"No, leave them," said Doug as a malevolent smirk spread across his face.

The crescent moon appeared through the cloud cover in the night sky as the figure moved with stealth across the yard to the side door of the warehouse. From a distance two almond eyes observed him closely in the dark. He crouched down and examined the lock. It was the same one as before. He shook his head, these people deserved to be robbed. The lock was picked in an instant. He opened the door and entered, letting it close behind him. The door glided against the frame and stopped ajar. Across the yard the dog stood up and crept slowly and silently towards the warehouse. The figure continued down the aisle shining his torch on the shelves once more, boxes marked socks, plates, lamps. Nothing he could take so far. He moved further along. A black nose appeared in the gap between the door and the frame and quietly prised it open. Sheeba entered and stood still, her head up alert and her ears pricked. The figure continued to examine the shelves: cards, whisky, mats. Either too bulky or too cheap he bemoaned. He concentrated the light higher up: towels, watches. Sheeba sniffed the air and began to move across the warehouse. What was that sound? The figure turned suddenly, shining the beam down the aisle. He remained motionless peering into the stillness. Must have been the wind or mice. He looked up at the box marked watches on the shelf high above. It was probably just within reach. He placed the torch on the shelf below, took off is balaclava and strained his arms upwards. Standing on his toes his fingertips could just touch the bottom of the box. He began teasing it forward towards the edge. Sheeba walked slowly to the end of the aisle. She observed the figure and moved silently along the narrow passage. The box inched its way to the brink, just a little bit more. He worked his fingertips along the bottom, edging it towards tipping point. One more step. The box came crashing to the floor. Suddenly, he heard the paws racing along the concrete towards him. Quickly he grabbed the torch and turned. The beam gave him a brief glimpse of the razor-like teeth before two powerful paws hit him in the chest and knocked him to the ground, sending the torch spinning out of his hand and extinguishing the light. In the darkness he could feel the dog's heavy body pinning him down and its breath on his face. He remained still, paralysed with fear as the nose sniffed his face and the sharp teeth brushed his cheek. Instinctively he closed his eyes. Then he felt it. A wet tongue lapped his chin and up over his mouth and nose. He groped around blindly for the torch. Finding it he switched it on and shone it into the dog's face.

"Sheeba!", he exclaimed stroking her golden fur affectionately. "I know a little girl who is longing to see you. Let's go home."

VAMPIRE

AUTHOR'S INTRODUCTION

References to vampires go back thousands of years, allusions to blood-drinking creatures can be found throughout the Bible in both the Old and New Testaments.

While there is no actual evidence of vampires existing, there is an abundance of belief in them. They gained particular popularity in Europe during the Great Plague, largely due to a lack of medical knowledge by the masses. As corpses decompose the skin shrinks, making it appear that the teeth and fingernails have grown longer. Additionally, as internal organs breakdown, a dark fluid can leak from the mouth, causing those unfamiliar with the process to interpret it as blood and ascribe it to having been drunk from the living. Disease has been a common instigator for vampire belief, throughout the nineteenth century the misunderstanding of tuberculosis led to vampire hysteria throughout New England.

Today vampires only appear in works of fiction, although there are a small minority who are convinced in their existence and constantly seek proof. In this tale Edward is such a person.

VAMPIRE

The young woman staggered drunkenly along the deserted street, she looked up at the full moon and the twinkling stars in the clear night sky. She felt the cold autumn air cutting through her skimpy blouse and pulled her jacket tight around her body. The moon disappeared behind the buildings as she turned into a narrow alley, the only light being provided by a dim lamp midway along. She looked through bleary eyes at the shabby, windowless edifices and graffiti marked doors. The buildings towered menacingly over her on both sides. She could smell the rancid stench of rotting waste as she lurched further down the alley, stepping through the discarded litter: old newspapers, stained food boxes and coffee cups, whose remnants dribbled out onto the discoloured paving stones. Teetering in her high heels she stumbled into a round, steel bin, knocking it to the concrete ground with a shattering crash. The lid rolled away with a continuous metallic ring. She supported herself leaning against the wall, watching as it slowed, circling on its rim with increasing speed and noise before reaching a crescendo and coming to rest. A sudden gust whipped through the alley scattering the rubbish, catching a small paper bag and raising it into the air. She gazed at it hypnotically as it danced in the night sky before getting stuck behind a pipe affixed to the grubby building opposite then pushed herself off the wall and continued walking unsteadily. As she approached the lamp it flickered causing her to stop and look up. It flickered again and extinguished casting the surroundings into a sinister darkness. She glanced anxiously around, she could just about make out the light from the street ahead. Cautiously she made her way towards it, conscious of the motionless silhouettes and eerie silence that surrounded her. A sudden rustling made the blood freeze in her veins, something scurried towards her. Her heart beat fast as she stood still and held her breath. She heard the hissing, the lamp above ignited for an instance on the black cat below. Its vertical slitted-eyes burned bright green as it stood, snarling, with its back arched before turning, racing down the alley and disappearing as the lamp extinguished once more. She sighed with relief and wiped her forehead. Without warning, she felt a heavy blow from behind knocking her to the hard ground. She felt the weight on her back pinning her down, paralysed with fear she was unable to cry out. Her hair was pulled to the side to expose her bare flesh, the last thing she would ever feel was the sharp pain on her neck.

Edward sat in front of his computer, the screen providing the only light in his bedroom. He glanced at the clock, 4.00am. In the street far below his apartment he could hear the cars passing in a seemingly endless procession despite the time. After four years of living here he had grown immune to the noises that constantly surrounded him: the baby crying above, the couples audible arguments below, the pipe knocking in the bathroom. None of these kept him awake at night. He starred at the screen. This is the reason he stayed up night after night into the small hours. The vivid title radiated in bold, gothic, crimson letters "THE VAMPIRE CLUB". He was transfixed by the perpetually appearing posts in a never-ending stream from people all over the world. Edward knew none of them personally but they all had one thing in common, the belief in vampires.

He removed his thick, black rimmed glasses and wiped the lenses with a cloth. His eyes felt heavy, maybe he should call it a night and get some sleep. He replaced the spectacles and moved the cursor over the log off button. Suddenly a new post appeared.

Buffy Cullen; Vampire killing in New York tonight.

Edward took his hand off the mouse and typed.

Ed the Undead: How do you know, Buffy Cullen?

Buffy Cullen: I live close to it..

Ed the Undead: Where is that?

Buffy Cullen: An alley just off East 12th Street, near 1st Avenue.

It was near him. There were frequent posts of killings but none had been conclusively proved to be committed by vampires. All he needed was one to establish their existence. He picked up his coat that was tossed on the bed behind and went out into the narrow hallway, made even narrower by the old, rusty bike propped against the wall. He squeezed past and opened the door before wheeling the bike into the corridor.

Fifteen minutes later he was pedalling down 1st Avenue. He thought about the names the members of The Vampire Club adopted. Buffy Cullen was clearly a reference to Buffy the Vampire Slayer and the family name of the vampires in the Twilight saga. He was quite pleased with his own, Ed the Undead, it rhymed beautifully, certainly a lot better than Edward Dunn. As he turned into East 12th Street he could see the flashing lights of parked patrol cars and an ambulance. A crowd assembled on the sidewalk was being kept back from the alley by two burly policemen.

Edward cycled slowly towards the throng, clambering to look behind the policemen at the scene in the alley. Further along he noticed the old woman who lived on his floor stood at the bus stop. She wore an old coat tightly fastened up to her neck with brass buttons, although one was clearly missing, and a shabby shawl covered her head. Over her arm was slung a large tatty canvas bag. Wrinkled grey stockings stuck out from under the coat slipping into grubby brown shoes. Edward turned back to the crowd who were becoming increasingly agitated.

"Is she dead?"

"I can't see, I think she is."

"You have to stay back!" boomed the cop.

"She's been killed by a vampire," screeched a woman with wild hair, a deranged look on her face.

"There's no such thing as vampires."

"Yes, there is. They walk among us at night, drinking the blood of the weak."

"Ignore her, she's been drinking the gin of the week."

A few people laughed uneasily, but not Edward.

"Make way!" ordered the cop. "They're bringing the body out."

The mob began to part, shuffling to the sides. Two paramedics appeared from the alley carrying a stretcher covered by a blanket. The crowd watched silently as they moved towards the ambulance. Suddenly the screeching woman lunged forwards and tore the blanket from the body.

"Look, I told you, the mark of the beast!"

Edward looked at the gaunt, lifeless face of the dead woman, her clothes torn and covered in blood and her neck horrifically mutilated. The paramedics quickly retrieved the blanket and covered the body while the cop restrained the now hysterical woman. They quickly put the stretcher in the back of the ambulance and sped away with lights flashing and siren blazing. The crowd began to dissipate as a bus pulled in nearby. Edward watched as the old woman ambled slowly up the steps.

"Wait for me!"

A young woman suddenly appeared, racing along the sidewalk, her long blonde hair flowing behind her as she ran. Edward smiled and raised his hand to wave but she mounted the bus with one bound and was gone. He watched longingly as the bus pulled out. As it past him he caught another brief glimpse of her before she disappeared from view. Quickly, he started pedalling home, he could cut through the park and be back at the block before the bus allowing him to spend a few precious moments with her. Her name was Lena and since she moved in last month his whole life had brightened, she was so beautiful with her long, golden locks, her flawless, pale complexion and thin ruby lips. She was tall and slim and moved so gracefully as though she floated on air. He recollected the night she moved in, how she smiled it him with her blue, sparkling eyes, a magical moment he would cherish forever. Her fingers were so long and elegant with immaculately manicured fingertips painted bright red. He had watched as she opened her apartment door, admiring her long, shapely legs below her short skirt before she disappeared from view. Every time he heard her in the hall he would come out

43

on some pretext just so he could see her. He had been taken aback when she told him she was a lap dancer. It made him angry to think of all those men leering after her.

The old woman turned in her seat to face Lena a few rows behind.

"That was a terrible tragedy, a young woman cut down in the prime of her life."

"Mmm," replied Lena nodding wearily.

"It's not safe for young woman to go out at night."

Lena rested her head back and closed her eyes.

"You should get a new job. That could easily be you lying dead in an alley."

"Or you," muttered Lena.

"Oh no, not me, dearie. I always carry this."

From her bag she produced a large knife. Lena opened her eyes slowly and looked at the long, sharp, gleaming blade.

"You carry that!"

"Everywhere I go," she said twisting it in the air and admiring its sleekness. "And I know how to use it."

Edward cycled quickly through the park arriving at the block just as the bus was stopping outside. He waited eagerly as the doors opened and Lena stepped down followed by the old woman moving slowly.

"Hi Lena," he greeted enthusiastically.

"Edward! You're up late."

"I went to see the murder in the alley, they say it was a vampire." he gushed excitedly.

Behind, the old woman looked up at them. Edward held the block door open as Lena glided sinuously into the lobby. He scurried behind letting the door slam shut in the face of the old woman.

"A vampire? Have you been on that site again?"

"They really exist."

"I'll be glad when they fix this elevator," bemoaned Lena clambering up the stairs.

Edward lifted his bike and struggled up while Lena walked just ahead.

"Do you know that old woman carries a knife?"

"Mrs. Brown?"

"It's huge, the blade must be a foot long."

Edward had always thought of her as being a bit strange, she had moved in only a few days after Lena. They arrived on the fourth-floor landing. In the corridor was a jet-black cat, it looked at them then arched its back and hissed. They stopped still watching the cat's claws extend and its eyes darken. Suddenly a ping came from the elevator and the door opened. The old woman emerged. She trundled forward, bent over and picked up the cat. They all stood looking at each other before the old woman disappeared into her apartment.

"The elevator must be fixed", observed Lena. "Oh, well, night Edward."

She opened her door and was gone before Edward could reply. He approached the elevator and stepped inside. That's strange, he thought, it had not been working for a month and he was unaware of any repair. He pressed the button for the ground floor. The door remained open and the elevator stayed motionless. He pressed other buttons but no response. Stepping out he looked mystified at the old woman's door.

The low sun streamed through the thin curtains and onto the black and white poster of Christopher Lee playing Dracula in an old film from the 1960s. In the small bed below, the bright sunlight caused Edward to stir. He strained his eyes open and squinted at his clock, 10am, time for work. He sidled from the bed to the desk opposite and turned on his computer. The room was cramped but functional with everything neatly in its place. He sat before his keyboard and typed. Working from home was great, it meant he could avoid commuting and because of flexitime he could pretty much work the hours he wanted. Once a week he would have to cycle across the city to the main office to give an update. As long as he was making progress with the computer programmes everyone was happy and they left him to his own devices. Before he started, each day he checked for any vampire updates. He wondered if his all-consuming interest was the reason the company allowed him to work from home, either way it was fine by him. He scrolled down the news feed. The murder last night featured heavily.

Buffy Cullen: Woman killed by vampire in New York last night had her heart ripped out.

Edward never heard that but he did re-collect that her clothes were torn and her torso was drenched in blood. He scanned the news headlines.

A young woman, identified as Mary Moodie, 20, was murdered last night in the East side of the city.

Nothing about a heart being torn out.

Ed the Undead: How do you know, Buffy Cullen?

Buffy Cullen: I was there, I saw, it was the work of a vampire.

Ed the Undead: Vampires do not remove the hearts of their victims.

Buffy Cullen: This one does and I know who it is.

Ed the Undead: Who?

No reply. Edward looked at her profile picture, a cropped photo of Bella from the Twilight Saga. No-one seemed to use a picture of themselves, not that he was one to talk as he admired his own profile picture, a black bat set against a full moon. He thought it was quite artistic. Suddenly a message appeared.

Buffy Cullen: Mercy Brown.

Edward was familiar with the story of Mercy Brown, she was believed to be a vampire in Rhode Island at the end of the 19th century. According to the legend, she was responsible for the deaths of her father, mother and sister by afflicting them

47

with a terrible curse. Medics believed that in reality it was tuberculosis, which they thought was also responsible for the death of Mercy Brown herself on 17 January 1892. However, the townsfolk of Exeter, Rhode Island would not accept this and exhumed their bodies. The other family members were decomposing skeletons but when they opened the casket of Mercy Brown they found her face flush and blood in her heart and veins. They immediately proclaimed her a vampire. Her heart was removed and burnt before they re-buried the body. He started typing once more.

Ed the Undead: What makes you think it's Mercy Brown?

A message appeared, *Buffy Cullen has left chat.*

Edward looked through the window into the darkness. He had been working all day but his mind kept wandering to the woman murdered in the alley. Was she really killed by the vampire Mercy Brown? He knew vampires existed but he needed conclusive proof to convince the rest of a sceptical world. A world where people embraced the safe security of denying the possibility of supernatural forces roaming among us. He determined to return to the scene tonight.

East 12th Street was unusually quiet as he rode along the deserted road feeling the icy wind on his face. Stopping on the sidewalk he looked into the desolate alley. A chill went down his spine. He dismounted and removed the light from the front of the bike. Slowly he made his way between the buildings shining the light all around him. Garbage covered the ground and the smell of rotting waste was pervasive. A rat scurried from under a discarded newspaper. Edward stood still watching as it sat up sniffing the air, its whiskers twitching before disappearing between two metal bins.   He continued down the alley until he arrived under the flickering lamp. This was where it had happened. He concentrated the beam on the ground. A dark red stain was clearly visible. Around it were a series of smaller red blemishes, obviously blood splats, thought Edward. He scanned the surrounding ground. Just litter and waste. He kicked a used coffee cup. As it hit the wall he heard a distinct metallic sound. Immediately he shone the beam in that direction. He moved cautiously towards it, crouched down and ran his hand over the ground, repulsed by the sticky liquid that clung to his palm. His fingers closed on a small object. He stood up and opened his hand, a brass button, just like the ones on Mrs. Brown's coat. Quickly he put it into his pocket and retreated from the alley. As he cycled back home his mind was racing. The old woman must have been in the alley. What was she doing there? She had only moved in a month ago and he believed she worked nights as a cleaner. Lena said she carried a large knife. No. it was too fantastic to believe that the old, hunched woman could kill anyone. Unless. Unless she was a vampire. Mrs. Brown? Mercy Brown?

He arrived at the apartment block and entered the lobby. Below the mailboxes he observed the old woman on her hands and knees combing the floor.   The door slammed behind Edward causing her to kneel up abruptly and face him. Slowly, she ambled to her feet and brushed her coat down.   Edward stared at the missing button. She followed his eye with her own.

"I was just looking for it, dearie," she croaked. "It must have fallen off last night, have you seen it at all?"

"No, no I'm afraid I haven't," lied Edward hastily.

"Oh, well, I'll have to get another one. It should be easier here in New York."

Edward watched as she traipsed slowly passed him and opened the front door.

"Where we you before here?" he called.

"Exeter, Rhode Island, dearie."

The door banged shut behind her.

Edward sat on the bus watching the rain drops zigzagging their way down the window. He had waited a few days before finally deciding to make the trip. The bus pulled into the terminus and he looked at the sign on the side of the building "EXETER, RHODE ISLAND." He picked up his holdall and stepped from the bus. He felt the rain landing on his head and looked up at the dark clouds above. At least the wet ground would make his task easier. He hurried to a nearby hotel.

Inside the small, dimly lit foyer he ruffled his damp hair. He looked around at the bare walls and this faded rug on the floor. An old man observed him carefully from behind a worn, wooden counter. Edward approached.

"I'd like a room for the night, please."

"Are you a reporter or tourist come to gloat?" he said accusingly.

"Pardon?"

"The town has been full of press and morbid gawkers, I thought it would all be finished by now."

Edward looked at him bemused.

"The dead girl, they all want to know about the dead girl."

"Dead girl?"

"We just want to forget about it, why can't you just leave us in peace?"

"I'm sorry, I have absolutely no idea what you are talking about."

"So, why are you here?"

"I just wanted a break from New York."

The old man scrutinised him sceptically.

"Very well, sign here, name and address."

Edward leant over and began writing in the open book.

"What's all this about a dead girl?" he asked as casually as he could.

"Terrible it was, murdered under a full moon, just last month, and only 18 years old."

Edward glanced up trying to disguise his interest.

"Found with her heart ripped out."

Edward kept writing, all the time listening intently to the old man.

"You know who's responsible, don't you?"

Edward stayed silent, his eyes on the page.

"Vampires."

Edward looked up into his manic face.

"You probably don't believe in vampires but they exist," raged the old man. "They have plagued Rhode Island for over 200 years and now they're back."

Edward finished writing and put the pen down.

"That's $80 up front."

Edward took the notes from his pocket and placed them on the counter. The old man turned the book towards him and took a key from the shelf behind.

"Enjoy your stay Mr. Smith."

Edward walked up the rickety stairs to a small, sparsely furnished room. A single iron framed bed was positioned against the wall. He dropped his holdall on top causing it to creak and approached the grimy, porcelain basin opposite, surveying the rusted taps. A high-pitched screech resonated around the room as cold water spluttered out. He threw some onto his face before taking the thin, worn towel from the rail below and drying, feeling the coarse material on his skin. So, a girl had been murdered and had her heart torn out. If Buffy Cullen was right that made two now. He locked the door and went back down the stairs into the foyer. The old man looked up as he entered.

"Can you tell me where the nearest library is please?"

"Turn left out of the hotel and you will find it about 200 yards along."

"Thank you."

Edward entered the rather modest library. A young woman sat behind the front desk but otherwise the room was empty. She smiled as he approached.

"Hi, you're the first person I've had in today," she beamed radiantly.

"Hello, I'm just visiting for a couple of days."

"Where are you from?"

"New York."

"We had lots from New York last month, and Pennsylvania and just about everywhere."

Edward guessed why.

"I'm looking for archive newspapers."

"At the back behind the history section."

Edward nodded in appreciation and began to walk away.

"You'll find it in Exeter News, 21 October," she called.

Edward stood in front of the rack and sifted through the stack of papers. It would probably be on the front page, a big story for a small town. He stopped and lifted one out; 21 October, headline: "GIRL MURDERED." He sat down at a small, round table and began to read.

Carrie Collins, 18, was found dead this morning in a disused yard. Early reports claim her throat had been mutilated and her heart cut out. Carrie was a bright girl who had recently graduated from Exeter High. This is the first time a heart has been torn out since Mercy Brown in 1892. Are vampires back in Exeter?

"The writer is a bit dramatic," said the librarian appearing behind him.

"You don't believe in vampires then?"

"Certainly not. It's the work of some psychopath. He could have been inspired by the belief in vampires I suppose. The people of Rhode Island, and especially Exeter, have a long history of vampire superstition going back to the 18th century."

"But why remove the heart?"

"It was believed that a potion could be made to cure those being made ill by a vampire. They would remove the heart of the supposed vampire, burn it on a pyre, and mix the ashes into an elixir to be given to the sick. The first case of this ritual was Sarah Tillinghast in 1799. Numerous other instances occurred over the following decades until the vampire hysteria stopped with the last case in 1892."

"Mercy Brown."

"Exactly."

"Where is she buried?"

"Chestnut Hill Cemetery."

Edward stood up and replaced the newspaper.

"Thank you very much."

"Anytime, come again."

Edward lay on the bed in the dark, outside the sun had set long ago. He listened to the silence as he steeled himself for the grisly task ahead, feeling a mixture of excitement and apprehension. What if he got caught, it was still a crime. Giving a false name and address to the hotel owner would make it hard for anyone to trace him. The old man could give a description but he intended to be on the early bus back to New York. The chances of them pursuing him there for such a minor infraction seemed remote. He pushed himself up from the bed and went over to the window. The street below was quiet and still. The sky was overcast but the earlier rain had ceased. He picked up the holdall and opened the door, closing it silently behind him. He moved stealthily along the corridor, down the stairs, across the dimly lit foyer and into the street. So far so good, he made his way along the deserted road towards the cemetery.

His heart beat fast as he crept between the tombstones shining a light on each in turn. He felt the cold breeze on his face and the only sound was his own feet on the wet grass. As he moved further into the graveyard the headstones became older, eroded by time, some covered with moss. It was an eerie place to be alone. Suddenly he stopped before a worn tombstone. The white masonry had become ravaged by the elements into a dark green discolouring. He read the epitaph:

MERCY L.

Daughter of

GEORGE T. & MARY F.

BROWN.

Died Jan. 17. 1892.

Aged 19 years.

He placed the holdall on the ground and unzipped the top. Furtively he looked around before reaching inside and removing the head of a shovel and two steel rods. He screwed the two steel rods together before inserting them into the shovel head and tightening it. The silver metal gleamed under the torch light. He stood before the grave, holding it firmly in both hands. This was going to be long, arduous work. With one sudden movement he plunged it into the ground, the head penetrating the wet grass. He pulled up the soil and dumped it to the side. An owl watched him high up on the branch of a nearby tree. The clouds began to part, giving a glimpse of the moon.

An hour later Edward wiped his brow as he breathed heavily. He looked down into the grave at the coffin. The owl hooted causing him to reel back in fright. He composed himself and lowered his body into the gaping chasm. Six feet down it was pitch black. He scrambled about blindly for the edge of the lid. Locating it he started to prise it open. The old wood creaked as it moved on its hinges. Edward's heart accelerated. What terrifying vision awaited him? He rested the lid against the side and reached up for the torch. He shone the beam into the casket. It was empty.

Day was breaking as Edward woke from his slumber. The bus hummed gently as it travelled down the highway. Edward looked through the window as it passed a road sign, "New York 20 miles". He thought about how long it would take them to discover the desecrated grave. No doubt there would be a search, the story would probably make the front page of the Exeter News. Not that he cared, he would be long gone and no-one would be able to trace him, besides, he had more important matters to think about; the vacant grave of Mercy Brown. There was something else, something the old man had said to him, *"terrible it was, murdered under a full moon."* The night of the New York killing there was also a full moon. Was there a connection? According to legend full moons were associated with werewolves not vampires, and yet.

That night Edward was back in his apartment He typed a private message on his computer:

Ed the Undead: I went to Exeter, Rhode Island.

He sat back and waited.

Buffy Cullen: Why?

Ed the Undead: I wanted to know about Mercy Brown.

Buffy Cullen: And what did you discover?

Ed the Undead: That she was believed to be a vampire and had her heart removed and burnt.

Buffy Cullen: You could have discovered that without going to Rhode Island.

Edward reclined back, he was not keen to admit to despoiling the grave.

Buffy Cullen: Obviously you had another reason for going.

Ed the Undead: I'm going to trust you. I went to Chestnut Hill Cemetery.

Buffy Cullen: To the grave of Mercy Brown?

Ed the Undead: I dug it up.

Buffy Cullen: Did you look inside the coffin?

Ed the Undead: Yes

Buffy Cullen: It was empty.

Edward exhaled heavily and ran his hands through his hair as he tossed his head back and looked at the ceiling. How does she know so much? He moved forward onto the edge of his seat and typed quickly.

Ed the Undead: How did you know?

Buffy Cullen: I know a great many things. I suspect you have another question?

Ed the Undead: Yes, I discovered a woman was murdered there last month and had her heart ripped out just like the New York killing.

Buffy Cullen: Carrie Collins, 20 October.

Ed the Undead: Yes, I also discovered that there was a full moon that night, the same as the New York murder.

Buffy Cullen: And you want to know the significance?

Ed the Undead: Yes.

Buffy Cullen: You know when Mercy Brown died?

Ed the Undead: 17 January 1892.

Buffy Cullen: Do you know the significance of that date?

Ed the Undead: No.

Buffy Cullen: What about this year: 22 August, New Bedford, Massachusetts or 20 September, Greenwich, Connecticut

Ed the Undead: They mean nothing to me.

Buffy Cullen: Find out. Pay particular attention to the lunar cycle.

Before Edward could reply a message appeared, *Buffy Cullen has left chat.*

Edward typed in a search, *archive newspapers*. Various sites appeared on the screen. He clicked on the top one. The site claimed to have newspapers from around America for the past 300 years. Edward typed in the search box *New Bedford 22 August 20XX*. The New Bedford Standard appeared on screen. In bold black letters the front-page headline read: "YOUNG WOMAN MURDERED". Edward read.

In the early hours of the morning the body of Holly Radatski, 21, was found in an alley just off Main Street. In a horrific attack her throat was mutilated and her heart torn out.

Edward frantically searched 20 September 20XX, Greenwich, Connecticut. The front-page of the Greenwich Time appeared, YOUNG MAN KILLED.

A mutilated body was discovered in the west side of the town early this morning. The man has been identified as Brad Kelly, 23. The police have confirmed his heart has been removed.

Edward sat back and contemplated what he had discovered; four young adults murdered with their hearts torn out. Three woman and one man. Clearly the sex was unimportant. He took up his pen and listed the killings in chronological order.

22 August, Holly Radatski, New Bedford, Massachusetts

20 September, Brad Kelly, Greenwich, Connecticut

20 October, Carrie Collins, Exeter, Rhode Island

19 November. Mary Moodie, New York

The murders were about a month apart. What had Buffy Cullen said, check the lunar cycle. He brought up the phases of the moon for 20XX. He scrolled through the dates in turn 22 August, full moon, 20 September, full moon, 20 October, full moon. It was incredible, all the killings took place on days when there was a full moon. He knew there had been a full moon in New York, he had seen it. Why were they all being killed under a full moon? Was a vampire really going from town to town in North East America? He had been interested in vampires since he was a young boy, almost 20 years, and he had never known any connection between a vampire and a full moon. He thought about Buffy Cullen. She asked him if he knew the significance of 17 January 1892, the date Mercy Brown died. He moved quickly to the edge of his chair and typed the date in the lunar calendar. The screen started buffering. Edward waited, his eyes never faltering from the monitor as his heart rate increased. He wiped his forehead and ran his hand through his hair. The screen was still; 17 January 1892, full moon.

He logged back onto The Vampire Club and sent another message.

Ed the Undead: Buffy Cullen I have the connection, Mercy Brown died under a full moon as did the others. But what does it all mean?

Buffy Cullen: That Mercy Brown lives among us as one of the undead, roaming from town to town. Every full moon she rises to kill a victim and rip out their heart to replace her own that was removed over a century ago.

Ed the Undead: I knew vampires existed. She could be anywhere now.

Buffy Cullen: No, she is still in New York.

Ed the Undead: How do we stop her from killing again?

Buffy Cullen: Wait for the next full moon and be ready.

Edward quickly returned to the lunar cycle, next full moon 18 December, less than four weeks away. He thought about the old woman across the hall. Could it be her? She had been near the alley off East 12th Street the night Mary Moodie was killed, she had been in Exeter, Rhode Island, the previous month when Carrie Collins was murdered. Lena said she carried a large knife. Then there was the peculiar way she could use the elevator when it was clearly broken, not to mention her strange cat. All he knew for certain was that three days before the winter solstice Mercy Brown would kill again.

Over the next few days Edward monitored Mrs. Brown. The only time he saw her was when she went out at night to her work. He had followed her a couple of times but everything seemed normal. In fact everything had gone quiet. He had not seen Lena at all. Even Buffy Cullen had gone silent. There were no more articles about the New York killing, or any unusual murders anywhere. It was as though everything had returned to normal, but Edward knew everything was not normal. He had circled 18 December, the date of the next full moon, on his calendar. He tried to concentrate on his work but his mind was full of thoughts about Mercy Brown and what would happen on 18 December. If Buffy Cullen was right the next murder would be in New York, but what could he do about it? He had to do something. Picking up his coat he moved decisively across the apartment and out.

When he returned, several hours later, he was carrying a long, brown paper bag. He put it on the bed and closed the curtains before going into the kitchen, returning with a meat cleaver and a thick bread board. Placing them on the ground and kneeling beside them he pulled a cylindrical piece of wood from the bag. He rested one end on the board at an angle and lifted the cleaver into the air. The blade cut into the bottom of the wood. He chopped again and again until wood chips scattered around the floor, Meticulously, he rotated the wood until he had shaped the end into a sharp tip. He held it up and admired the wooden stake. Now he was ready for the next full moon.

Edward woke up early and looked at the calendar, 17 December, tomorrow was the day. The closer it had gotten, the more distracted he had been. His work had suffered and unsurprisingly he had been summoned to the office. In the hall all was quiet. He looked at the closed door of Mrs. Brown. Was she inside lying asleep in a coffin at this very moment? He pressed the elevator button. Nothing. How long did it take to fix he marvelled as he made his way down the stairwell. In the lobby he approached the mailboxes. On the table below was a large brown parcel. He opened his mailbox, empty. At least no bills he thought as he focused back on the package. He turned it to face him and read the label, Mrs. Brown. What could it be? He picked it up, whatever it was it was quite light. Something she was going to use tomorrow night? Edward put it back and walked into the street, in less than 48 hours he would know.

As expected he was severely reprimanded by his boss and made to work in the office until late. By the time he got back to the apartment block it was dark. He glanced towards the mailboxes, the package was still on the table. Furtively he looked around, he was alone. He scrutinised the package again. Swiftly he crossed the lobby, snatched it up and raced up the stairs. His heart raced as he opened his door and closed it quickly behind him. He placed it on the desk and went into the kitchen returning with a knife. Carefully he sliced the tape until he could open the carboard flaps. The object inside was protected by a polystyrene cover. Tentatively he reached inside and lifted it. He sighed with relief as he looked at the wicker cat basket. Perhaps he was wrong about Mrs. Brown, would a vampire really be buying cat baskets? He lifted it out of the box. The brown wicker encircled a soft white fleecy cushion. He was about to replace it when he noticed a sheet of paper face down on the bottom of the box. He took it out, turned it over and read, *Delivery Note, Luxury Cat Basket, for Mrs. M. Brown.* Mercy Brown? Edward placed the delivery note and basket back in the box. He closed the flap and used some fresh tape to seal it. No-one would know it had been unwrapped. He moved to his door and eased it quietly, listening intensely for any sound. He stepped into the hall. Suddenly he heard a ping from the elevator. The blood froze in his veins. He was statuesque, paralysed with fear, the package in his arms. His mouth was dry and his eyes bulged wildly as he watched the elevator doors open. A woman stepped out.

"Lena?"

"I left something in my apartment."

"I thought the elevator was still broken?"

"They must have fixed it. What's in the package?"

"Quick, come in," he gestured.

"I've got to go to work, Edward, I'm already running late."

"It's only for a minute," he implored. "It's important."

"Oh, very well, but just for a minute."

They entered his apartment and closed the door.

"What is so vital?"

"This", he said holding up the package.

"And what's that?"

"A cat basket."

"I'm going," said Lena slightly annoyed and walking towards the door.

"It's not that it's a cat basket, although it is a cat basket," he flustered. "It's who it's for?"

"Who is it for?"

"Mrs. Brown."

"You bought Mrs. Brown a cat basket?"

"No, it's not that, it came for her today. I'm not making myself clear, it's for Mrs. M. Brown."

Lena looked at him blankly.

"Don't you see, it's for Mrs. M. Brown", he said excitedly emphasising the "M"."

"I have no idea what you're talking about Edward."

"Mercy Brown, she's the vampire Mercy Brown."

"I'm going."

"Wait, I can prove it", he rambled quickly. "She is going around the states killing people and taking their hearts. She was near the alley the night that girl was murdered, last month she was in Rhode Island when another girl was killed."

Lena strode to the door and put her hand on the handle.

"And tomorrow night she will kill again."

Lena stood still and turned her head.

"How do you know?"

It will be a full moon, she always kills under a full moon.

"What are you going to do?"

"I intend to follow her tomorrow night and eliminate her from the world."

"How?"

"With this."

Edward proudly held aloft the wooden stake."

Lena looked at it.

"You watch too many vampire movies, Edward, good night."

She opened the door and was gone.

The sun had set long ago, Edward sat at the desk with the lights off. Today was the day, 18 December. The curtains were open allowing the light from the full moon to partially illuminate the room. He looked at the computer screen and a message he had typed hours ago.

Ed the Undead: Buffy Cullen, I know who Mercy Brown is. I will end it tonight.

There had been no reply. His front door was ajar and he had strategically placed a mirror at an angle so he could see into the hall. The holdall lay on the ground beside him. He looked inside at the sharpened wooden stake before zipping it closed. His body shuddered as he thought about the task that lay ahead. What would tonight bring? Suddenly, he heard a door open. He looked intensely into the mirror as Mrs. Brown ambled down the hall towards the elevator. Swiftly grabbing the holdall he moved to the door and peered through the crack. The old woman entered the elevator. He strapped the holdall over his back, wheeled the bike out and raced down the stairs, arriving in the lobby just in time to see her leave the building. Outside the air was cold and dry. Further down the road he observed the old woman standing at the bus stop, her coat all buttoned up and the tatty canvas bag was draped over her arm. The bus arrived and she got on board. He watched her through the window, walking calmly down the aisle before taking a seat. Looking at her sitting patiently on the bus Edward found it hard to believe she was really a vampire. The bus pulled out and he followed at a discreet distance.

On and on they went, the bus trundling along First Avenue before turning into East 12th Street. It stopped outside the same alley where the girl had been killed. Edward watched as the old woman dismounted and vanished into the dark alley. A shiver went down his spine as he looked up at the bright full moon. Slowly and steadily he approached the entrance, leaning the bike carefully against the wall and removing the holdall. He placed it on the ground and unzipped it before reaching inside. His hand closed decisively around the wooden stake and he lifted it out. He looked apprehensively into the dark, quiet alley. Midway along the lamp flickered. He began moving tentatively into the darkness, the stake raised over head, its sharp tip pointing forwards. His heart beat faster with each step as he became aware of the sound of his own rapid breathing. The lamp stopped flickering and shone down from above revealing the garbage strewn ground and surrounding grimy walls. Edward kept moving forwards, his eyes darting left and right. He stopped below the lamp and lowered the stake. Where could she be? Suddenly, the lamp extinguished casting the alley into darkness. Edward felt an icy gust of wind cutting into him, then the terrifying sound of rapidly approaching footsteps getting closer and closer. A heavy blow hit his chest, knocking the stake out of his hand and hurling him roughly to the hard ground. He felt the weight on his body and two hands of steel pinning his wrists down. In the dark he was unable to see, he struggled in vain but his assailant was too powerful. Above, the lamp flickered back to life and he looked into the monstrous face looming over him. Not as he knew it, but horribly distorted, the hair wild, eyes burning fiery red and the grotesque mouth exposing the fangs.

"Lena?"

"I am Mercy Lena Brown." she hissed as she lowered her mouth towards his neck.

He tried to fight his way free but it was no use. He felt the teeth on his exposed flesh and closed his eyes tight.

"AAAARRRRGH1"

The blood curdling cry filled the alley. He felt his wrists being released and opened his eyes. The vampire's arms were thrown open, the body and head arched backwards and through the chest blood was dripping from the tip of a blade. Edward looked at the anguish on her contorted face as she lowered her head. She slid off the blade as she slumped forward onto Edward, behind her stood the old woman, her hand firmly clenched around the blood-soaked knife. He pushed the lifeless body away and sat up dazed.

68

"Is she dead?" he murmured.

"Quite dead."

"But how? I thought you had to drive a wooden stake through the heart."

"This knife is no ordinary knife, it is an ancient, sacred artefact that has silver running through the blade. You have a great deal to learn."

"I don't understand," he murmured. "Who are you?"

"I am a vampire slayer, you know me as Buffy Cullen."

"You're Buffy Cullen?"

"I have been tracking Mercy Brown for four months, ever since I realised she was responsible for the killing in New Bedford."

"Why didn't you kill her before, I saw you here last month, you could have killed her on the bus or at her apartment?"

"Her apartment door was secured with extra chains and bolts, she knew who I was, just as I her. I always adopt the name of the vampire I am tracking so they know I am after them My cat always hissed, warning me when she was near. As for the bus, for one thing others could see and for another she was too powerful for me to take on face to face, maybe 20 years ago, but not now, I needed to distract her."

"With me?"

"I'm afraid so."

"But if you're getting older who will fight the vampires now?"

"My successor has been selected."

"Who?"

"Your training has already begun."

A DARK WINTER'S TALE

AUTHOR'S INTRODUCTION

I first had the idea for A Dark Winter's Tale several years ago. It is quite common for a writer to have a notion long before the story is actually written. Sometimes I will wake up in the middle of the night, racing to jot down the kernel of a thought before it slips into oblivion. I always make a note whenever inspiration strikes, some never come to anything, forever destined to remain a scribble on a piece of paper. However, others ferment and mature in the mind like a fine wine. Such was the case with this tale.

What would you do if you found yourself trapped with a serial killer? This was the premise with which I started. It might be that no rational decision is possible, the fight or flight instinct automatically springing into action. There is a much over looked third reaction, namely, freeze. This is, of course, of no practical use at all. But can you imagine the sheer terror of being confronted by a dangerous psychopath; bigger, stronger and totally in control, freezing would be perfectly understandable.

The young woman in this story did not freeze, but did it help her?

A DARK WINTER'S TALE

The chilling wind raged ferociously through the intimidating trees surrounding me making the bare branches high above tremor and howl as the rain drove down without mercy through the darkness. I had been scrambling desperately over the bracken, lost on the hill, for what seemed an eternity. I looked up, just about able to see the outline of the branches towering over me and the black clouds shrouded above. The icy raindrops fell on my face and I quickly lowered my head, pulling the hood of my anorak tighter. I continued to make my way blindly with no idea of direction, I figured if I kept heading downwards I would eventually come to the road. My mobile phone was useless for light as the battery had died, despite John giving specific instructions to us yesterday.

"We are going on a lesser-known route up Ben Gulabin in a circle that will bring us back to Glenshee," John had informed the small group.

This would be my first hill-walk and I was very much looking forward to it, though in truth, I would have preferred to go in summer rather than the middle of winter. At least it would be a break from studying for a few days.

"Make sure you bring your mobile phones, just in case of an emergency and that they are fully charged. Especially you, Sarah," he had added looking at me.

Everyone had laughed, my reputation for being a bit scatty was well-known. Only last week I had left my college assignment, that had taken me three months to complete, on the bus. Fortunately, my name and Edinburgh University were written on the cover and I got it back from my dismayed tutor a few days later.

Despite that personal warning, I had been so excited to go hill-walking in Glenshee that I had completely forgotten to charge my phone. Now here I was detached from the group and unable to phone anyone for help. No doubt John and the others would be trying to contact me. Initially, when I realised I was cut off I had waited, but once the rain started and darkness fell I decided to try to find them. That was stupid of me, I should have remained where I was. I had no choice now but to make my own way back to the hostel and meet them there.

I fought my way through the bracken, cold and wet, I could feel the rain seeping through my anorak and my hands were freezing, my thin gloves offering little protection from the harsh winter conditions. As the trees became sparser I was aware of a clearing ahead, my heart lightened, at last, the road.

I felt instant relief as my sodden boots touched the tarmac. But which way should I go to get back to the hostel? I had no idea. Looking right and then left, both ways were pitch black but either would surely lead to some sort of civilisation, a village, or at least a farmhouse. I turned right and started walking, the rain still pouring down but I felt safer now.

On and on I trudged along the winding road, the rain turning to hail in the increasing cold and bouncing off my anorak. Suddenly, I could see the bend ahead being illuminated, getting brighter and brighter. Then I heard a sound that brought immediate joy, the low hum of a car engine. As it turned the corner I could see the headlights on full beam lighting up the trees on either side of the road. I raised both hands and started waving and shouting frantically. Closer and closer the car came. I moved to the side, still waving furiously. To my horror the car sped past me and disappeared around the bend. I was devastated, my arms slumped to my side and I stood motionless with my head bowed. I felt like crying. Once more I was alone in the darkness. The engine faded as I looked into the emptiness, I was left desolate with the sound of the hail beating down and the wind whipping around me. As tears began to well in my eyes the curve began to illuminate. Another vehicle, perhaps this one would stop. I scarcely dared to hope. The road brightened, I could hear the engine, then saw the headlights. The car was approaching slowly. I leapt into the middle of the road waving and shouting, desperate to be seen. The beams shone on me as the car stopped in front, it was the same one. I rushed to the passenger door, grabbing the handle and yanking it open.

"Thank you so much for coming back, I didn't think you had seen me," I gushed as I got in.

I quickly closed the door to keep the rain out, extinguishing the light inside. I looked at the driver and could just about make out his large silhouette in the darkness.

"It's so cold and wet out there," I added fumbling with the seat belt. "You are my saviour."

I tugged it hard but it refused to move.

"I think it's stuck."

"Allow me," said the driver in a deep gravelled voice.

He reached up and switched on the light. For the first time I could see him clearly. He was a big man, middle-aged, with a bald head and a black grizzled beard that was greying over his

75

chin. His eyes were dark and sunken and he was wearing a shabby. brown, leather jacket, torn on one sleeve, over a crumpled grey shirt and dirty blue denim jeans. As he leant forward and reached across me I was struck by the smell of stale cigarette smoke that pervaded his clothes. I was conscious that his body was touching mine as he wiggled the belt before pulling it slowly over me and securing it in the buckle. It felt uncomfortably tight across my chest but I did not like to complain, I prayed it would be a short journey. He turned the light out casting us into darkness and the car moved off. We sat in silence, the only sound being the hail beating down on the roof.

"I was hill-walking and got lost," I said.

He made no reply, his hands fixed firmly on the wheel and his eyes looking straight ahead.

"We're staying at the hostel in Glenshee," I continued. "Is this the way to Glenshee?"

Still he made no reply, his unnatural silence becoming increasingly unnerving.

"Can we have the radio on?" I asked eager to mask the uncomfortable silence.

He did not answer but reached forward to the radio and turned the dial.

"...next up, a classic from The Eagles.."

My mind turned to recent events, it was strange, he passed by me on the road, turned around, picked me up and was now heading back in the same direction. Where was he going?

The car was filled with the haunting music of Hotel California. The guitar picked out each note, made more chilling with the accompanying hail above.

ה "... *On a dark desert highway, cool wind in my hair*

Warm smell of colitis, rising up through the air... " ה

"This is a dangerous place for a young woman to be by herself at night," he said.

There was something unsettling in the slow deliberate way he spoke each word.

"Oh. I'm not by myself," I replied hurriedly. "There's a big group of us. They are waiting for me right now back at the hostel."

I looked towards the windscreen, through the wipers sweeping the water away furiously, out into the darkness. The headlights illuminated the winding road and trees that seemed to surround the car. The seatbelt was taut across my body and seemed to be getting tighter. Who was this man beside me? I would never normally get into a car with someone unknown, even less so at night on an isolated road. Yet here I was, pinned in a car with a total stranger.

"Is this the way to Glenshee?" I asked again wringing my hands as I waited for a response.

He was silent again, why would he not tell me?

♫ *"...You can check out any time you like,*

But you can never leave...".♫

Abruptly, the car screeched to a halt, causing the seatbelt to cut into me as I was propelled forward. My heart was beating fast and my mouth was dry as I looked at him in terror, my eyes wild with fear. Without a glance in my direction he opened his door slowly and got out, closing it firmly behind him. I watched him through the windscreen as he walked down the road in front of the car, the rain pelting off his bald head. This was my chance to escape. I grabbed the buckle in both hands, furiously pressing the button while I pulled on the strap. It was stuck fast, outside I could see him bending down in the middle of the road. When he stood back up he had a thick branch in his hand. I yanked the seatbelt more violently.

"Open, damn you!"

I tried wriggling my body out of the strap but it was too tight across my chest.

"We interrupt this programme to bring you breaking news. The serial killer Joseph Kerenski, known as Joe Le Taxi, the taxi killer, who escaped from Shotts Prison last week, has been spotted in the Glenshee area. Police have advised all local residents to be alert, he is known to be armed and dangerous and should not be approached."

I stopped struggling, Joe Le Taxi, I knew that name. He had been responsible for the abduction and murder of five women, luring his victims by masquerading as a taxi driver. Once inside his cab he drove to a secluded spot and killed them, mutilating their bodies in a frenzied attack with a large jagged-edged

78

knife. Suddenly, the driver's door flew open, his giant body filling the doorway. I froze, my eyes never faltering from the thick branch held firmly in his enormous, hairy hand. He lifted it above his head, I was unable to make a sound although I wanted to scream. He smiled before turning and tossing it to the side of the road.

"Lucky we didn't drive over that, it must have been brought down by the wind," he said getting back in the car. "It could have broken the axle."

As he shut the door I heard a click beside me. My door had locked.

The car pulled away into the darkness on a seemingly never-ending road. Not another vehicle was to be seem, I was alone.

"...and now it's time for the news..."

He reached forward and turned the radio off.

"I hate the news," he said coldly.

I sat pensively in the dark and silence. Beneath my feet I could feel papers and scrunched, plastic cups thrown carelessly to the floor. I needed to get away, but how? I studied my surroundings. Immediately, my whole body froze. I do not know why I had not noticed it before, beside the steering wheel sat a meter, the digital orange numbers displaying £10.

"Oh my God, this is a taxi," I murmured.

"Don't worry, I'll take good care of you."

The blood froze in my veins, this could not be happening to me. I was overcome with terror looking frantically around, I had to get away.

"You're shivering," he said with a menacing grin.

Keep calm, Sarah, I told myself, I had to keep composed, it was my only chance to survive this nightmare.

"I'm cold," I said trying to disguise the tremor in my voice.

I glanced sideways at him through the wet hair that was bedraggled across my face. He was staring at me with his dark, lifeless eyes.

"Dry your hair," he commanded. "There's a towel in the glovebox."

I reached slowly forward, my hand trembling, and opened it. A light came on inside and I could see it crammed with rags and a ball of string. I rummaged around and found a small, white towel wedged at the back, As I tugged out it something heavy fell to the floor at my feet. I bent down and picked it up, I just sat there transfixed looking at the object. My heart seemed to have stopped and I was unable to breathe. In my hand was a large knife with a sharp, serrated blade. I felt a big, rough hand grip mine and rip it aggressively out of my grasp.

"I'll take that," he said brusquely. "That's my hunting knife."

I felt the colour drain from my face as I watched him place the knife in the door pocket. I could see the leather handle sticking threateningly up.

"Close the glovebox," he ordered.

As I closed the glovebox plunging the inside of the car into darkness again I buried my face in the towel. Tears were forming in my eyes. I longed to be home safely in my bed. I would plead for my life, that's what I would do. Beg him not to hurt me. I wiped the tears away from my face with the towel then placed it over my head and began to slowly rub my wet hair. Surely, he would take pity on a young girl. I was so frightened, I could not stop trembling. My mind was racing. He would not take pity on me, he had already killed five girls just like me, he had not shown them any mercy, slashing at them while they no doubt sobbed and pleaded. Stabbing and cutting them with his jagged knife until they stopped breathing.

The car weaved its way through the country lane. I was conscious that the rain was no longer beating down on the roof and the wipers were still. The wind seemed to have subsided too, the only sound was the gentle humming of the engine. I finished drying my hair and put the towel down, I would only have one opportunity. From deep within myself I began to summon the courage I was going to need to survive. Steadily, I moved my right arm to my side until it reached my thigh. Inch by inch I moved my hand towards his seat. He was looking straight ahead, unaware that my fingers were now touching his leather jacket, my fingertips extending slowly, searching. My heart was beating so fast I could almost hear it as my breath reduced to a murmur and my body was still. My fingertips brushed down his jacket until they found what they were looking for, the hard, plastic, seatbelt buckle. I took a firm grip of it and placed my thumb softly on the button. I focused on the road ahead, we were on a straight section. The car accelerated, the headlights illuminating a sharp bend in the distance. I waited and waited, my hand tensing on the buckle. Closer and closer the car sped towards the curve, I had to choose the optimal moment to act. I would only get one chance. The headlights illuminated the trees on the bend as we prepared to turn. It was now or never, I steeled myself and pressed down hard on the button. As the seatbelt fired across his body I grabbed the handbrake and pulled it up with all my might. The tyres screeched on the wet road sending the car into a skid. He grappled with the steering wheel turning it left and right trying to regain control but the car careered of the road. The lights illuminated the thick trunk of tree and we ploughed head on into it. I was jolted violently forward with the impact causing the seatbelt to tear into my body almost cutting me in half as I watched him shoot forward, his head smashing against the windscreen causing it to crystallise before he collapsed back in his seat. I pressed my hands against my burning chest, it was sore but I was alive. I looked at the lifeless figure slumped beside me. On his forehead I could see the deep gash from which blood was streaming down his face. I flopped back with relief, I had survived. Suddenly, I heard a voice. I froze. No, this could not be possible.

"Calling all drivers."

I ran my hands through my hair as I tilted my head back and let out a huge sigh of relief, it was just the taxi radio control.

"In the last few minutes the police have announced that they have re-captured Joe Le Taxi."

SWIPE RIGHT

TWIST IN THE TALE SHORT STORIES

The sun blazed through the office window onto the rows of plastic chairs and the anxious faces within. All eyes focused on the over-head projector casting a bright white square onto the screen behind. The office was usually tense, becoming heightened at the end of the month. They waited nervously for the boss, all except one. Alex Tanner stood assuredly next to the coffee machine, the rays shone on his sharp navy suit and crisp white shirt. His jet-black hair was swept back onto his collar and he grinned confidently. Despite being in his forties he still had a firm, chiselled jaw and a muscular physique.

The door opened decisively and an old man carrying a bundle of papers strode purposefully across the room to the window. He yanked on the cord casting the room into an ominous darkness.

"Take your seats and we'll get started," he instructed pressing the switch to provide some soft lighting.

Alex Tanner sauntered to the front row and sat down.

George Bailey had built the Bailey Estate Agency from nothing to make it number one in the area. He surveyed the assembled group, revelling in their nervousness. Life for him was all about money and power, they had given him a nickname, King George, from which he took great gratification. He loved the feeling of omnipotence, he knew he had the God-given power to make or break people. A thin gold chain hung around his neck suspending a small crucifix gently against his tie.

"God has blessed us with a stupendous month," he boomed. "Sales up on the previous period, mainly due to the sale of the Wilson Park property."

He exchanged a tacit nod with Alex Tanner who smiled smugly. On the opposite end of the front row a young woman in a red skirt suit looked at him scornfully, her eyes burning with ire. Alex raised his cup in her direction as the blood boiled in her veins.

Bailey rambled through all the statistics while the group listened eagerly.

"Now we come to a very grave issue," he declared solemnly scanning the faces with an icy glare. "It has been brought to my attention that someone has been engaging in activities that I can only describe as smut."

The employees shifted nervously in their seats and looked furtively at each other, all but Alex Tanner who sipped his coffee in a relaxed manner.

"I will not have this filth in the workplace," he shouted slamming his finger onto the projector. On the screen appeared a young woman posing provocatively in high-heels, black stockings and suspenders, with her skimpy white blouse open giving a tantalising glimpse of her tight cleavage as she pouted at the camera with her ruby red lips.

A small, thin man at the back of the room went pale as Bailey marched to the window and pulled the cord flooding the room with light.

"Yes, you, Dale Peterson," he raged pointing accusingly at the young man. "This was the picture found on your computer."

"I was just buying a present for my wife," he blurted in desperation.

"Silence! It's the picture of a God-fearing harlot!"

"No! It was just to buy the lingerie for her birthday. I was pressed for time due to working on the Wilson Park deal."

"So, it's not enough that you look at perverted filth but you also try to muscle in on another man's achievement."

"I was helping Alex with the sale. Tell him, Alex," he implored.

Alex Tanner shrugged his shoulders.

"I don't know what you are talking about Dale."

Dale slumped in his seat and looked at him incredulously.

"Clear your desk and get out," condemned Bailey.

Dale stood up slowly and walked dejectedly towards the door with his head bowed. Alex Tanner smiled maliciously as the door closed behind him.

"I will not stand for obscenity, it is an offence to God. Anyone who is found with this sordid muck can expect the same swift treatment," threatened Bailey.

The group shuffled uneasily in their seats as he scrutinised them judgmentally

"Right, that will be all, back to work."

Bailey collected up his papers and marched out of the room. The rest frantically gathered their belongings, hurrying out. Alex strolled leisurely to the coffee machine and calmly pressed the buttons.

"You really are a piece of work."

He looked around. The young woman in the red suit stood up and tossed her long blonde hair back.

"What are you talking about now, Monica?"

"You know exactly what," she said caustically, brushing the skirt down over her shapely legs as she approached him slowly. Even in her high-heeled stilettos he still towered above her small, svelte figure.

"You know Dale and I were integral to the Wilson Park deal."

"King George doesn't see it that way."

"Only because of the lies you feed him. I know it was you who told him about the lingerie picture on Dale's computer."

"I suggest you calm down Monica, why don't you go and take a slug from the hipflask you keep in your car?"

"You really are a bastard," she seethed clenching her hands tightly into fists.

Alex smiled arrogantly, picked up his coffee and walked nonchalantly towards the door.

"You'll get what's coming to you, Tanner, you just see if you don't!"

She sped quickly from the room and down into the carpark. Dale was putting a small box of meagre possessions into the back of his car.

"Dale!" she called racing across and giving him a hug. "It won't be the same without you."

88

"Ten years I was here," he said ruefully gazing up at the building. "My first full-time job."

"You'll get another. I'll get that Tanner back if it's the last thing I do."

He smiled weakly.

"I can help you there. He has his own dark secret."

"Go on," said Monica eagerly.

"He goes on a dating site."

"The bastard, not only does he screw us over but also his wife."

"It's a very special site."

Monica's eyes lit up in anticipation.

"It's a BDSM site," he continued.

"Masters and slaves?"

"Exactly. It's called Bondage Dating."

"He likes to take charge of willingly subordinate women? That doesn't surprise me at all, the arrogant prick."

"No. He likes to be dominated."

Monica stood open-mouthed in stunned disbelief.

"This is gold," she gushed excitedly. "Why didn't you go to King George with this? I'm going to, this will be the end for that pompous, self-important ass."

"There's a problem."

"What?"

"We can't prove it's him. He goes by the name Castus and in all the pictures he is wearing a full head mask."

"Like a gimp mask?"

"Something like that."

"So, how do you know about it"

"He got drunk on a night out a few months ago and boasted about it, saying how he could get away with anything right under the nose of King George."

Monica remained silent deep in contemplation while Dale got in his car and started the engine.

"If you think of anything you can let me know."

"I will, bye, Dale," she shouted as he drove away.

The sun was beginning to set as Monica sat in her car across from the glass fronted office block. She glanced at her watch, 5pm. In her hand she held a folded sheet of paper. How much longer would she have to wait? The front door opened and a procession of people in suits began pouring into the courtyard towards their cars. Monica scanned their faces looking for one in particular. The employees continued to stream out. More and more engines were being started and a line of vehicles headed for the exit. Monica chewed her lower lip tensely as the car park thinned out and less and less people emerged from the building. She wondered if she even had the right place, racking her brains to remember. Suddenly the door opened and a small woman came out. Monica looked at her dowdy, beige, quilted coat coming down over a long, grey, pencil skirt that stopped well below her knees. The woman scurried across the yard with small, rapid steps and her head bowed timidly. What did that arrogant knob see in her she pondered looking at her plain face and long, lank, mousy brown hair. The woman approached a small mauve hatchback and disappeared inside. The engine started and the car crawled slowly to the exit. Monica pulled out and followed as the car dawdled down the road. This was Helen Tanner, Monica had only met her once, some months ago at a company function, but she had a good memory for faces and recollected how she had told her where she worked. She was impressed with herself she had remembered as the conversation had been incredibly tedious, this woman seemed to have nothing in her life but her laborious office job and her idolisation of her husband. Thinking about it, that was probably the appeal for him, no doubt he lapped up her misplaced hero worship. Being ten years younger also probably appealed to his vanity.

The mauve hatchback turned into the supermarket, even the car was a putrid colour, thought Monica. She parked a short distance away and watched as Helen scuttled into the shop. Monica opened her door and picked up the note. She walked quickly to the hatchback and slipped the paper under the windscreen wiper. That would set the cat among the pigeons she mused strolling back to her car with a smile of satisfaction playing on her ruby lips.

Helen Tanner ambled out of the supermarket struggling to control a bag-laden trolley with a wonky wheel. Monica watched as she strained to keep it moving in a straight line. Eventually she arrived at her car and loaded the shopping into the boot before getting in the driver's seat. A few seconds later she re-emerged, reached under the windscreen wiper and removed the note. She opened it and read. Monica observed the puzzled expression on her face. Helen glanced around the carpark before getting back in the car. Monica was satisfied, she started the engine and drove away. Inside the car Helen stared intensely at the piece of paper and read it again. *Check out Bondage Dating website, member Castus.* It was hand written in blue ink. She scrunched it up and tossed it on the floor of the passenger seat before driving away.

As she moved down the road the ball of paper rolled around the floor. She turned into the driveway of a large, modern, detached house and stopped. Two trips were needed to unload all the shopping. She returned a final time to get her handbag from the passenger seat. Opening the door she lifted it and looked at the crumpled paper with uncertainty. Tentatively, she reached down and picked it up.

Inside the house she carefully stored the groceries before smoothing out the note. What did it mean? She glanced nervously at her watch, Alex had said he was working late tonight. She went upstairs to the study and turned on the computer. As she waited for it to come to life she stared at the wrinkled note, questions racing through her mind: Who had written it? Why had they sent it to her? What did it mean? The screen illuminated and she typed hurriedly in the search box, *Bondage Dating*. The page filled with results. She clicked the top one. The screen filled with the image of a dimly lit dungeon, the name BONDAGE DATING was emblazoned across the top in bright red gothic letters. Below was a muscular man dressed only in tight lycra shorts and a black rubber mask covering his entire head. His toned arms and legs were stretched out across an X-shaped wooden cross, his ankles and wrists secured to the frame by leather cuffs. Beside him stood a voluptuous woman in a short, tight red PVC dress which hugged her shapely body. High-heeled leather boots came up above her knees. She looked sternly at the captive young man while she flexed a thin cane in her hands.

Helen flinched with revulsion, she had no interest in this perverse depravity. She moved the cursor over the close screen button and stopped. Once more she read the note, *member Castus*. She looked back to the screen. Along the top were several selections. She pressed "Members Section " Rows of pictures filled the screen, men in gimp masks, women wielding whips, at the bottom was a box labelled "Search Members." Helen typed "Castus." A photo appeared of a black rubber hood stretched tightly over a man's head, with a blindfold over the eyes and a red ball gag strapped to the open mouth. Why would someone think she would be interested in something so disgusting? Beside the picture was a brief profile, Helen forced herself to read.

Professional male into Femdom, love being tied up and roleplay. For other pictures click on gallery.

Helen clicked. A new picture appeared. The man was standing, naked except for a leather body harness. The black straps came up over his shoulders and extended down over his hips and a netted chastity belt covered his crotch. Despite the degrading attire Helen had to acknowledge that he did have a good physique. His skin was smooth and his body well-toned. She stared at the picture, a look of anxiety spreading across her face. She moved her head closer to the screen. On his right thigh was a small brown mole. She recoiled away from the screen and covered her mouth, a look of horror in her eyes, Alex.

It was late when Alex pulled onto the driveway. He looked in surprise at the empty space where Helen's car would normally be and the house completely in darkness.

"Helen?" he called opening the front door.

No response. He switched on the light and walked down the hall to the kitchen. The house was eerily quiet. On the table he noticed a small note. He picked it up and read, *Gone to Nina's.* He scrunched the piece of paper up and tossed it in the bin, what melodramatic crisis was she experiencing now he fumed clenching his teeth together hard. Yet again running off to her sister who would no doubt rant about him at length. He went into the lounge and poured himself a large whisky from the crystal decanter before sinking down in his armchair. There were more important things to think about than Helen's histrionic tantrums. It had been a good day, King George had given him all the credit for the Wilson Park sale and he had got rid of Dale ensuring there could be no comebacks. There was still Monica but she could not do much to him by herself and she knew it. Beside he could now work on getting rid of her, it would be easier now she didn't have her little buddy. He smiled smugly and took a big swig from his glass, allowing the whisky to swill around his mouth before swallowing it. Putting the glass down he walked across to the bureau and removed a folder. He returned to his chair and opened it, "Regent Hill Mansion." For him this was the Holy Grail of deals, a luxurious mansion over-looking the entire town, complete with swimming pool, hot tub, snooker room, tennis court and best of all, a huge master bedroom with a magnificent, antique four-poster bed. A millionaire's dream, a playboy's paradise, and absolutely impossible to sell. It had been on the books of the Bailey Estate Agency for over a year and not one serious buyer.

Sure, plenty of people wanted to waste his time snooping around the home of the country's most notorious gangster but no-one would dare to buy it. He took another sip from his glass. Who could blame them, they didn't want to end up at the bottom of the river. Enquiries had all but dried up over the past few months, it just sat there, uninhabited, dominating the town, a sinister reminder of a man destined to spend the rest of his days in prison. He had to sell it, he just had to, it would mean partner for sure, not to mention the huge bonus on offer. There had to be somebody out there who would buy it, there just had to be.

Helen was slumped over the dining room table, her face buried in her crossed arms, gently sobbing. Opposite her a younger woman in a tight vest and shorts stared aghast at an open laptop.

"I told you he was no good," she proclaimed running her hand through her short auburn hair. "What sort of name is Castus?"

"It's the name of one of the slaves with Spartacus," whimpered Helen looking up through her teary eyes.

"What a ridiculous name."

Nina stood up and stretched her slim, athletic figure.

"It's time you left him, Helen, the disgusting pervert."

"But I love him," wailed Helen.

"He treats you like a doormat and like a fool you let him. I'll go around there right now and tell him you are leaving."

"No, Nina!" pleaded Helen wringing her hands. "Can I stay here tonight?"

"Of course you can, but that is not a permanent solution. What are you going to do, Helen?"

"I don't know, I need to think."

"Nothing then, as usual," condemned Nina placing her hands firmly on the table and towering over her sister. "If you don't do something this time Helen then I will."

The following morning Monica sat at her desk in the open plan office. She observed Alex across the room talking loudly on the phone.

"It's a beautiful property, rare to have it on the market, you had better view it quick."

Monica watched as he reclined in his large leather chair and beamed confidently. He was his usual arrogant self, so much for her note causing trouble for him at home.

"This afternoon, yes I can meet you there at 2pm."

She would have to take more drastic action.

King George emerged from his office and strode into the middle of the room waving a piece of paper agitatedly in his hand.

"I have just received this letter regarding the Regent Hill Mansion," he raged. "They are threatening to take the property off us if we cannot sell it by the end of the week."

He glowered around at his staff most of whom immediately averted their eyes, looking down nervously at their shoes or staring blankly at their computer screens.

"We haven't had a single viewing for over three months," he continued to rant.

"It's because of Big Ken and the threats," said a young man timidly.

"So, the previous owner was a gangster, so what? He's in prison and won't be coming out any time soon."

The young man lowered his head.

"Do I need to sell it myself" he yelled, his face going red with increasing anger. "Show you all how it's done? I was the best in my day, I could sell snow to the Eskimos."

"I'll sell it."

"I knew I could rely on you, Alex. This is a real salesmen," he proclaimed loudly. "A man after my own heart. Sell this and I'll make you partner."

King George put the letter on his desk and walked briskly back to his office. Monica watched as Alex picked up the page and smiled conceitedly. She would have to take more drastic action.

"Thanks for meeting me for lunch, Monica."

"No problem, Dale, I was glad to get out of the office."

They sat at a discreet table in the small bistro.

"Any new developments?" he asked casually sipping his orange juice.

"King George has conditionally offered Alex partner, that will make my life intolerable."

"What's the condition?"

"That he sells the Regent Hill property."

"I think you're safe."

A waiter appeared, placing a salmon dish in front of Monica and chicken before Dale.

"I hope so, Dale. You should have seen him boast to King George how he would sell it."

"No-one has put in an offer for that property and no-one will unless they want their legs broken."

"I suppose your right, nobody has been there for months, it's all but abandoned," replied Monica cutting her salmon fillet. "King George himself was bragging about his past glories, I got the impression he would love to sell the property himself. Two arrogant peas in an arrogant pod."

"Alex might have bitten off more than he can chew, he over-estimates his abilities, he only sold the Wilson Park property because of us. This one could come back to bite him, you know how King George despises failure."

"I'd love to see the look on his stupid face if he got sacked."

Dale nodded knowingly as he chewed his chicken. So, would he.

For the second day in a row Alex arrived home to find Helen's car missing and the house cast in total darkness. He went in, not even calling her name, no doubt she was still at her sister's. Momentarily, he wondered what had brought on the crisis this time before turning his mind to the Regent Hill property. He had spent most of the afternoon and evening speaking to his contacts and potential buyers but to no avail. The strain was beginning to show. He poured a large whisky and took a big gulp. What if he couldn't sell the mansion? He took another huge swig. This could not be a failure, he was Alex Tanner he reminded himself forcefully, he did not know the meaning of failure. He finished off the remains of the whisky and re-filled his glass. Best to get his mind off it for a while. He went up to the study and turned on the computer. If he could not sell the property he would be a laughing stock, he, Alex Tanner, would become an item of ridicule, the office clown. The screen came to life and he typed on the keyboard. Gone would be his chance of ever making partner, he would be the thing he dreaded most, worthless, a failure. He lifted the glass to his mouth and drank heavily, beginning to feel the numbing effects of the alcohol. On the screen his profile appeared, Castus. He gazed at the picture, this was exactly how he felt as he looked at the harness enslaving his naked body, he was pathetic, he was a loser, he deserved to be punished. He raised the glass to his lips. Suddenly, the computer bleeped, someone had swiped right, he had a message. He put the glass down and opened it.

Megaera: Hi, I saw your profile, looks like we have a lot in common.

It was rare for a woman to contact him. He opened her profile page.

MEGAERA, 30 years old

Hi, I'm new to the BDSM scene. I love being dominant, tying up, whipping, all boundaries respected. I would like to meet a nice slave to fantasise with and have role-playing fun.

Love Megaera.

There was just one picture, a slender woman wearing a long black robe, high-heeled boots and leather gloves. She had long, flowing, golden hair and was wearing a silver mask with two tiny eye slits. It covered her forehead and nose and extended down her cheeks to her jaw on both sides framing her scarlet lips. He looked at her location, same city as him, he replied.

Castus: Nice photo.

Megaera: I like yours too xx. I'm new to this site. Have you been here long?

Castus: A few months. So you are into BDSM?

Megaera: Yea, I love dominating a willing slave xx

Castus: I need to be dominated, I'm a very bad slave.

Megaera: Mistress will need to punish you.

Castus: Yes mistress.

Megaera: Tie you up

Castus: Yes mistress.

Megaera: Whip your naked flesh

Castus: Yes mistress.

Alex finished off his drink, this was exactly what he needed.

Castus: Do you meet?

Megaera: I've not met anyone yet.

Castus: Would you like to?

Megaera: Sure, that is the purpose of the site, I guess lol xx

Castus: How about tomorrow afternoon?

Megaera: Ok xx

Castus: I know a little motel, just perfect for discreet assignations.

Megaera; No, not somewhere public.

Castus: I could visit you.

Megaera: No, not at my place.

Castus: Where then?

Megaera: Somewhere nice, private, secluded.

Alex looked at her picture, he had to meet her. Maybe it was the alcohol but an idea sprung into his mind, an exciting idea, a dangerous idea.

Castus: I know just the place.

Alex drove along the long winding tree-lined driveway, the radiant sun shining on him in his open-top convertible. He pulled up at the large oak doors and looked up at the mansion. If he couldn't sell it, it might as well serve some purpose. He entered and climbed the marble staircase to the master bedroom. He looked at the huge king-size bed framed between the four solid metal posts. Perfect. He opened the window slightly to allow in the fresh air and closed the curtains, causing the room to dim. Glancing at his watch he quickly removed his clothes, admiring himself in the full-length mirror. He tightened the leather harness around his naked body. It had been a while. Downstairs he heard the front door close and the sound of stiletto heels crossing the wooden floor. He pulled the rubber mask over his face and got onto the bed. The footsteps increased in volume as they resonated on the marble stairs, approaching slowly and deliberately. Alex lay back in anticipation. The footsteps drew nearer and nearer. He sat up and focused on the bedroom door as it opened gradually, inch by inch, until Megaera appeared with the light from the landing behind her. She stood still and silent in the doorway, the living embodiment of her picture. Alex breathed quickly as his heart raced. Looking at her robed, slender body, the high stiletto boots making her taller than she actually was. Her golden locks flowed around the silver mask. She moved deftly towards him stopping at the edge of the bed. Alex looked at the coiled whip hanging from her belt and lay back submissively as she reached under her robe and removed two pairs of steel hand cuffs. He stretched his arms out behind to the posts. She moved around the bed and secured each wrist in turn to them. Alex panted as she detached the leather whip and unwound it until it dangled from her gloved hand. He closed his eyes as she ran the whip slowly and sensually over his bare skin. His flesh tingled as he felt the sinuous leather glide over his body. Megaera placed

102

the whip down on the bed. Alex's mind raced in anticipation of what delights would come next. He felt the cool breeze from the open window on his naked body, but that was all. What was she doing? He opened his eyes and lifted his head to see.

"No photos!"

Megaera was stood at the end of the bed pointing her mobile phone towards him. The flash went off.

"I said no photos!" he snapped angrily.

The flash went off again.

"Let me up!" he ordered straining to free himself from the handcuffs in vain.

Megaera produced a small key from her robe and moved around the side of the bed. She reached down quickly and ripped the mask from his head.

"What the hell are you doing!" he raged.

The flash went off yet again.

"You're crazy," he yelled writhing helplessly on the bed. "Untie me!"

"I think King George will be interested in these pictures."

Alex stopped struggling and remained still. That voice. She was trying to disguise it but it was familiar to him. He concentrated his mind.

"It's going to be hard to make partner now. I think, in fact he'll almost certainly fire you. You're finished, Alex."

Alex was startled, she knew his name. He regained his composure as Megaera showed him the photo on her phone

"I'll deny it's me, it's easy to fabricate fake digital pictures."

"Good point."

Megaera pressed the buttons on the screen and Alex could hear the dialling tone.

"I'll put it on speaker phone for you."

That voice was sounding increasingly familiar despite the obvious attempt to conceal it.

"Good afternoon, Bailey Estate Agency, how may I help you?"

"Hello, I'm interested in viewing the Regent Hill mansion."

"I'm afraid the person who is dealing with that property is out of the office at the moment. I can arrange an appointment for tomorrow."

"It needs to be today, I'm going away on business early tomorrow morning and won't be back for some time"

"One moment, please."

Alex remained motionless and apprehensive on the bed. A voice boomed through the speaker filling him with terror.

"Good afternoon, this is George Bailey, owner of Bailey Estate Agency, I believe you are interested in the Regent Park property and would like to view it today."

"Yes, as soon as possible, I have been looking for a property like this for some time."

"Certainly, I will conduct the viewing personally. When would be convenient to meet?"

"I can meet you at the mansion in one hour."

"Perfect."

"I'm particularly interested in the master bedroom."

"I will go to the property right now and check the master bedroom."

"Thank you, Mr. Bailey, see you soon."

Megaera switched the phone off and moved to the window. She threw open the curtains and placed the handcuff key on the sill. Alex watched her as she walked towards the door.

"Who are you? Why are you doing this?

She turned around.

"Revenge is a dish best served cold."

She reached up and with one swift motion removed the mask and golden hair. Alex looked into her face in stunned disbelief before he smiled resignedly with a hint of admiration and respect in his eyes.

"Kudos, a brilliant job. Congratulations on the voice and disguise. I should have recognised you, small and slim. I didn't think you had it in you, Dale."

STRANGER IN THE NIGHT

TWIST IN THE TALE SHORT STORIES

Ross Conrad had dreamed of being a policeman ever since he could remember. As a child he loved playing cops and robbers, he was, of course, always the cop. He had a dome police helmet which was never off his head, a plastic truncheon and toy hand cuffs. The other children used to call him Bobby Conrad. He loved the police shows on television from The Bill to CSI. He had no time for the amateur detectives of fiction such as Sherlock Holmes or Miss Marple, these were fantasy creations who did not exist in real life and frequently painted the genuine police as fools instead of the highly skilled professionals that Ross knew them to be.

Ross grew up to be tall and slim with light brown hair that he always kept short and tidy. He was keen to leave school as soon as he could and join the police, but his parents insisted he went to university first, so he did. He did not overly care for being a student, but he did meet Becky. Becky was quite reserved when he had met her in first year. She was small and slim and Ross had been drawn immediately to her long flowing chestnut hair and coy smile. He was not very confident with girls but had plucked up the courage to ask her for a coffee. They talked easily on their date as though they had known each other for years and became an item on the campus. Ross loved Becky and Becky loved Ross in a way that only young 19-year-olds can. They married a month after his graduation. It was a double celebration because Ross was accepted as a police cadet the same day as the wedding. They moved into a little semi-detached house together on a modern housing estate and Ross's life was going to plan. He shone at police cadet training school and was assigned to a station and given a partner. His partner and mentor was PC David McAdam, a highly experienced officer in his forties. McAdam lived with his wife Angela in a neighbouring street to Ross in a similar type of house. Angela was McAdam's second wife, small and slim and had long flowing hair like Becky. She was considerably younger than

109

him, in fact about the same age as Ross himself. Living so close was quite advantageous as McAdam could pick up and drop off Ross in the patrol car.

On a cold dark winter's night as they were on patrol they came across a car seemingly abandoned in a deserted country lane on the outskirts of the city. The lane was narrow and surrounded by trees and bushes. There were no streetlamps with the only illumination being provided by the full moon above. McAdam slowed down as they passed and looking across could just about make out the silhouette of a figure in the driving seat. He pulled in just ahead of the lone car and turned the engine off. It was so quiet, eerily quiet, no sound from anywhere. No wind in the trees, no small animals moving in the bushes, nothing, just silence. He glanced in the rear-view mirror. The figure was motionless. Both officers got out of the patrol car to investigate. The night was so quiet and still they could hear each footstep as they walked and see the breath in front of their faces. As they approached the car Ross was struck by its strange shape. It was very low like a sports car but pointed at the front and slightly raised at the rear. Ross was a car enthusiast and knew all the top sports makes but this was something different to anything he had seen before. As they neared Ross could see that the car had no lights or registration plate. What kind of strange vehicle was this? They reached the car and bent to look in the driver's window. Inside was a tall, scrawny man dressed in a long, black robe with fine, long, white hair down to his waist. He remained still, just facing forward. McAdam knocked on the window with his knuckles breaking the deathly silence.

The stranger moved his head slowly and looked at the officers. Ross observed his thin, bony face and sharp pointed nose. There was something unusual about it, almost unnerving. He was struck by his pale, gaunt skin and his sunken, lifeless eyes. It reminded him of a dead body he had once seen and sent a chill down his spine. The window began to wind down.

"Good evening sir. Can I ask what you are doing out here alone at this time of night?" enquired McAdam in his usual authoritarian manner.

"Is it against your laws to be out alone at night?" replied the stranger

"Is this your car sir?"

"I've never understood this strange concept of ownership that you have."

"Where's the registration plate/"

"I have no need for registration plates."

"Show me your licence," demanded McAdam getting increasingly annoyed with the stranger's obtuse responses.

The stranger ignored him and looked at Ross. he could feel his deathly eyes burning into his own.

"So, you're Ross Conrad."

He was surprised to hear the stranger speak his name.

"Or do you prefer Bobby Conrad?"

Ross had not heard this name since he was a young boy.

"Living out your dream of being a policeman and married to the lovely Becky."

Ross was unnerved that the stranger knew so much about him.

"Who are you?" he blurted out in desperation.

"The question is not who I am, but what I am."

McAdam could see the increasing tension in the young officer's face.

"Name!" he barked through clenched teeth.

"You would not understand my name."

"Address!"

"I am from no place known to you."

"I've had enough. Show me your licence right now or you are going to spend the night in the cells."

"I don't require a licence," laughed the stranger derisively, throwing his head back.

"I'll play along," said McAdam switching his manner to patronise the stranger. "Where are you from?"

"I am not of this world."

"So, you're an alien?"

"Something more than that."

"A superhero? Do you have superpowers?" asked McAdam mockingly.

"Perhaps you could call them powers."

"Give us a demonstration of your powers."

"You won't like it if I do."

"I'll risk it," smirked McAdam.

The stranger closed his eyes, a look of concentration on his face. He was still and solid, like rock, as though transfixed.

McAdam laughed and looked at him incredulously. He glanced at Ross. Ross was not laughing, he looked worried. This weirdo had really gotten to him, thought McAdam, time to put a stop to this charade. Just as McAdam went to speak the stranger suddenly opened his eyes.

"It's done."

He looked at the officers with his eyes seemingly more dead than before.

"Your wife is dead."

"Becky!" Ross cried out.

"Out of the car right now!" commanded McAdam angrily.

The stranger remained still. Ross was paralysed with desperation. McAdam had to snap Ross out of his state.

"PC Conrad get him out of the car right now!" he ordered.

Ross's eyes were wild and panicked.

"PC Conrad get him out of the car. NOW!"

Ross moved forward, frantically grabbing the door handle and wrenching it open. The stranger just sat there with an unnatural calmness. Ross reached in and grabbed him by the arm. As his fingers closed around the stranger's bony arm his mind went into a raging whirl. He felt as though he was racing across the land with the surroundings rushing past him in a blur. As everything stopped spinning and came into focus he found himself outside the house. In the street he saw a parked ambulance with its blue lights flashing. The house was in total darkness. His body seemed to elevate and glide through the front door into an eerily quiet hall. At the end of the hall he saw the kitchen door. He floated towards the end of the passage. The door opened and despite the darkness he could make out the figure of the body laying still on the floor with the long flowing hair covering the face.

"Becky!" he wailed.

His vision blurred and his mind was spinning again. He was conscious of being back in the lane with McAdam pulling him back.

"It's Becky. I've got to get to Becky" he said trembling and attempting to break free from McAdam's grip.

"Go and sit the patrol car," said McAdam trying to maintain control of the situation.

Ross felt the grip release and ran to the squad car, stumbling as he did so.

"You," hissed McAdam at the stranger. "You just stay here. I'll be back."

He reached in and took the keys out of the ignition. The stranger remained just as silent and still as always.

McAdam slammed the door shut and strode briskly back to the patrol car, opened the door and got in. Ross had his mobile phone clenched to his ear, a look of increasing terror on his face as the phone rang out again and again. McAdam kept his attention on the car behind as he spoke.

"What the hell is wrong with you? You need to pull yourself together boy."

"I saw her. She's dead."

"No-one is dead."

"I saw her. There's no answer from her phone. I need to get home."

"No! Enough!" shouted McAdam. "I'll tell you exactly what we are going to do. We are going to take that nutter to the station and he can spend the night in the cells."

He reached across and shook Ross roughly by the shoulders.

"Repeat it back to me. We are going to take him back to the station."

"We are going to take him back to the station," mumbled Ross.

They got out and walked back to the car. McAdam unclipped his handcuffs ready. He took a firm grip of the car door and opened it.

"You're going to......"

He stopped speaking abruptly. The car was empty.

"Let's go," implored Ross, panic taking over again.

"No. He must have got out."

"You were looking at the car the whole time," said Ross in desperation.

"He must have got out," repeated McAdam with less certainty.

"You know he never got out. But he's gone. Becky. I need to get home."

McAdam said nothing. He turned and walked hastily to the patrol car. They sped back to the city in silence save for the constant ringing out of Ross's mobile. Over and over again, a haunting ringing in the darkness with no-one to answer. Arriving outside the house Ross raced out before the car had fully stopped leaving McAdam alone and silent.

The house was in darkness, not a single light to be seen. Ross ran to the front door. He yanked the keys out of his pocket and searched frantically for the right one. The bunch spun on his palm and fell to the floor. He knelt down in the dark and feverishly swept his hands over the cold ground. His mind raced, where were they? He felt the metal, bolted up, put the key in the lock and threw the door open.

"Becky!"

No response.

"Becky!"

He pressed the light switch but the house remained in darkness. Despite his increasing terror he ran down the hall to the closed door at the end. He put his hand on the knob and stood motionless. For the first time since he had met the stranger he paused to think. He knew what he was going to find when he opened the door, he had already seen it. A life so idyllic was going to be shattered in seconds, his whole future lain to waste. He released the handle and took a step back. Ross did not want to see behind the door, he desired to turn and run, yet he could not. He stood paralysed with fear and dread, not wanting to move forward, unable to move back. A force within him, outside of his will, moved his hand back onto the door knob. It compelled him to turn it. The door began to open. Gradually it opened, inch by inch. The inside was pitch black, he could not see, he did not want to see. His eyes scanned the floor. The invisible force within him moved his trembling hand slowly up towards the light switch. His finger paused over it and he closed his eyes.

Click.

The light flickered then stabilised, he could feel the brightness on his eyelids. Slowly he opened them, the kitchen was empty, he let out a huge sigh of relief. Suddenly, he felt a hand on his shoulder. He spun round. He let out a wail and flung his arms around her.

"Becky! My Becky!"

She held him tight as tears rolled down his cheeks.

"Where were you?"

"In the basement, a fuse had blown taking out most of the lights."

"I thought I'd lost you forever."

"What's the matter?" she asked tenderly caressing his hair. "Why is David McAdam sitting in the car outside?"

"David! I forgot about David. Come with me," he said taking her by the hand and walking quickly to the front door.

He waved to McAdam with his arm around Becky, holding her tight. He had never known such intense emotion. McAdam pulled away as they closed the door.

He was pensive and unsettled as he drove the short distance home, he had been watching the deserted car the entire time. How did the stranger get out? He had just disappeared into thin air. Who was he? As he turned the corner into his street, outside his house he saw the parked ambulance with its blue lights flashing.

TWIST IN THE TALE SHORT STORIES

SNAKE

TWIST IN THE TALE SHORT STORIES

"So, the matter is settled, the winner will be promoted and the loser will be sacked."

He reclined magnanimously back in the plush, cream, leather chair and puffed on a thick Cuban cigar, the epitome of success and accompanying opulence. The tip burned bright orange as he drew the smoke into his mouth and scrutinised the two men stood obediently before the large mahogany desk. He lifted the slender object laying on top by the leather grip and ran his fat, stubby hand down the carbon shaft to the angular head.

"This is the key to success," he purred caressing the grooves on the blade. "The real sport of kings. The man who does not know golf does not know business."

Luke Grainger looked at the club in his boss's hand masking his disbelief. He turned his head to the side and observed the twisted smile and cruel glint in the eyes of Simon de Vere.

"Life is a continual competition, a survival of the fittest with the lame falling by the wayside," continued the boss placing the club back on the desk. "Tee off time will be tomorrow 9.00am sharp."

He motioned the men away with a dismissive movement of his hand. They paused in the corridor and looked at each other.

"May the best man win," said Luke extending his hand.

De Vere gripped his hand firmly and gave one vigorous shake.

"Indeed," he sneered.

Luke stood in the doorway and looked up at the clear Florida sky feeling the warm afternoon sun on his face. He put his key in the lock and turned it.

"You're home early," said a soft voice, approaching and kissing him tenderly on the cheek

He looked down pensively at her distended stomach, not long to go now. What would happen if he lost his job, he thought as he bit his lip.

"What's wrong Luke?" she asked, immediately noticing the concern on his face and squeezing his hands in hers supportively.

He took a deep breath as he looked into her worried eyes.

"By this time tomorrow I might be out of work," he said resignedly.

"What do you mean," she replied horrified. "They can't fire you after everything you have done and all the long hours you have put in."

"Caroline, they will if I lose tomorrow."

"Lose tomorrow? What are you talking about?"

"That's the deal; promotion or the sack."

"How?" she asked perplexed and concerned. "Come and sit down."

She led him by the hand to the sofa. They sat down and faced each other with their knees touching and their hands still clenched.

"Tell me what's going on," she implored.

122

He looked at her loving eyes that made him ashamed of the affection he did not deserve.

"Tomorrow I must play golf against Simon de Vere. The winner will be promoted, the loser fired."

"They can't do that," she gasped horrified.

"They can and they will. This is the reality of the "American dream," Caroline, win or lose, where the weak are left to die."

"It must be illegal."

Luke shook his head despondently.

"You haven't played for years," she added desperately.

"I know," said Luke releasing her soft hands and getting up silently.

"Where are you going?"

"To practice," he replied quietly as he walked slowly across the room.

In the hall he opened the cupboard door, reached into the back and removed the golf bag. He wiped the dust from the top and put it over his shoulder. Opening the front door he turned around and looked back. She was leaning against the wall with her head to one side and tears in her eyes.

"Don't trust de Vere," she murmured.

Luke nodded silently closing the door behind him.

Simon de Vere sat up in the bed and took a long draw on a cigarette while observing the contours of the nubile, naked body beside him. She looked up adoringly resting her head on her hand.

"Do you have to go so soon?" she pleaded.

"Tomorrow is the day I get my promotion," he replied letting the smoke drift from his mouth as he spoke.

"You could stay the night."

"No, I need to get back."

"To her, she hissed bitterly."

"You knew the situation when you started this," he said coldly extinguishing the cigarette and slipping from the bed.

She watched as he quickly dressed and headed for the door.

"Will you come tonight?" she implored.

"I'll ring you," he replied closing the door behind him.

Luke stood alone on the teeing off area for the first hole, above the sky was clear and the warm sun brightly illuminated the rich green grass as he looked down the tree lined fairway. He put on his cap to protect his eyes, the golf bag strapped across his back with the sun's rays glinting off the freshly cleaned clubs. His watch showed 8:55, where was de Vere? Suddenly a buggy approached with two men. Luke recognised de Vere reclined in the seat. They stopped and de Vere got out.

"You're using a buggy?" enquired Luke surprised.

"Of course, sorry it's only a two-seater," he said maliciously. "This is Eddie."

A portly, middle-aged man was removing the golf bag from the back of the cart.

"He'll be caddying for me. Eddie toss a coin for who tees off first."

Eddie removed a coin from his pocket and flipped it in the air.

"Heads!" boomed de Vere.

"Heads it is."

"Right I'll tee off," he said placing his tee and ball as Edie handed him the driver.

He took a practice swing and addressed the ball. A clean metallic crack filled the air as the ball ascended ever higher.

"Good shot," complimented Eddie.

Luke placed his ball on the tee with his club in hand and looked down the fairway. The trees and thick grass on the sides were to be avoided. He kept his eye on the ball and swung. Contact was clunky, he watched the ball veer into the trees.

"Oh, bad luck," smirked de Vere getting onto the buggy with Eddie and trundling down the fairway.

Luke returned the club to the bag and slung it across his back. A bad start he thought pensively but there was a long way to go. He entered between the trees and scanned the thick grass for his ball. Not too bad, it was on a flat piece and the green was not blocked by the trees. He drove the ball out landing it near the green. As he put his club back and moved away in the long grass he was being carefully observed by two black vertical slitted eyes.

Despite Luke's bad first shot the score was level after 3 holes. Luke teed off on the fourth hitting a beautiful drive down the middle of the fairway. De Vere gave a huge swing hooking the ball towards the trees. He jumped into the buggy and drove down with Eddie ahead of Luke. As Luke strode down in the summer sun he observed them searching in the long grass between the trees. The grass was so thick in parts that anything could be concealed. De Vere brushed his club over the blades flattening them and carefully scrutinising the ground. The two vertical eyes remained deadly still watching every move, the lithe body tensed, ready.

"It came in somewhere by here," shouted Eddie.

De Vere kept sweeping the ground as he got closer and closer to the hidden vertical slitted eyes. The eyes fixed on him, never faltering as he took each slow, deliberate step. For an instant, the forked tongue flashed from the mouth and the ridged scales coiled tighter. De Vere drew nearer, the triangular head slowly rising, the body tensed as he came into range. The sinister eyes targeted.

"Over here!" called Edie.

De Vere turned and retreated as the snake relaxed but ever watchful.

"It's a bad lie," commented Eddie observing the ball in a thick clump of undergrowth.

"We'll soon fix that," replied de Vere subtly kicking it onto a flatter piece of grass. "Give me a 7 iron."

Eddie remained silent and handed him the club.

After 14 holes the sun was climbing higher in the sky and Luke walked casually in the warm rays leading by one shot. He was hitting the ball confidently and felt calm and relaxed as he observed his ball on the edge on the green. In contrast de Vere had landed in the steep walled bunker. Luke anticipated increasing his lead with just 3 holes to play. Eddie removed the sand wedge from the bag as de Vere wrenched it angrily out of his hand, the tension visible in his face. He stomped into the bunker and took an aggressive swing next to the ball spraying a plume of sand into the air.

"You're not supposed to take a practice stroke in a bunker," protested Luke.

De Vere scowled at him, Eddie stayed silent, Luke decided to let it go, he was winning and had a better position. De Vere lashed his club through the sand sending the ball spiralling into the air. It thudded onto the green, Luke watched in horror as it trickled towards the hole and dropped.

"Great shot!," praised Eddie as De Vere strode across the green with an arrogant sneer on his face and retrieved his ball.

Luke crouched down behind his ball and looked at the hole, a slight slope to the right. He stood up and placed his putter behind the ball, if he could make this he would maintain his one-shot lead. The ball rolled towards the hole, it looked good, Luke bit his lip anxiously. At the last second the ball veered

127

away and came to rest at the side of the hole. Luke stroked it in, they were level with 3 holes to play.

On the 16th De Vere placed his ball on the ground and looked at the short par 3. He took his 9 iron and swung confidently. The ball sailed high into the sky and landed on the green

"Good birdie chance," observed Eddie.

De Vere smiled smugly and looked at Luke. Luke placed his ball on the ground, the pressure was mounting. He focused on the ball, if ever he needed a true shot it was now. The club drew high behind him then descended rapidly hooking the ball viciously to the left into the undergrowth. De Vere smirked maliciously. The buggy trundled down the fairway while Luke ambled between the trees and the thick grass. He pushed his foot through the undergrowth as he scanned the ground meticulously. This was concerning, if he could not find his ball he would lose another shot, and with just two holes to play that might prove fatal. As deep concern preoccupied his mind he never heard the barely audible hiss ahead. He moved slowly forward scrutinising every blade of grass. He could feel his life draining away, Caroline, the baby, how could he pay the mortgage? The catlike eyes observed him silently, never wavering as he drew closer. Luke continued sweeping his foot through the long grass oblivious that he was not alone. The triangular head began to slowly rise, inch by inch. Luke moved nearer and nearer as the scales coiled tighter and tighter. Suddenly, Luke stopped, he was aware of the deadly, unnatural silence. He could sense something and remained motionless, something was there. Nothing moved, Luke felt a cool breeze on his face as he peered into the undergrowth. His heart began to beat faster as he tentatively stepped forward and began to lower his head. What was that? Suddenly, it thrust forward and he looked in terror at the open mouth and razor-sharp fangs. Quickly moving back he stared wild eyed at the penetrating vertical slits and the deep devouring mouth. He retreated rapidly, almost falling as he scrambled frantically out of the undergrowth. As he approached the others his face was ashen and he was breathing heavily.

"What's wrong with you?" demanded de Vere.

"It's a snake," he panted.

"Did you find your ball?"

"Didn't you hear me, there's a snake in there."

"There are no snakes around here," scoffed de Vere. "If your ball is lost you will need to use another and drop a shot."

"We need to abandon the game and tell someone," said Luke desperately.

"So, that's it, you want to quit because you are behind and going to lose."

"Look, there's a dangerous snake on the course."

"Dangerous?," quizzed de Vere sceptically.

"What kind of snake?" asked Eddie.

"I don't know, it was brown with yellow rings, eyes like a cat and a white mouth."

"Sounds like a Cottonmouth," appraised Eddie. "You do get them in the marshes around here but I've never seen one on the course."

"Well, there is one now."

"Show us," sneered de Vere doubtfully.

"I'm not going back in."

"Just show us the place."

The three men made their way to the trees and undergrowth.

"It's just by that big tree, concealed in the long grass."

Eddie removed a club from the bag and stealthily moved between the trees.

"Don't break my 4 iron," instructed de Vere.

Eddie surveyed the ground carefully as he moved silently forward. He concentrated intently, his eyes fixed on the long grass. Luke and de Vere watched on as he went deeper into the undergrowth. He stopped abruptly and stood statuesque. His eyes penetrated the long grass as he slowly and silently raised the club above his head. There was a deathly quiet. The club raised higher into the air as Eddie tightened his grip. Time seemed to be standing still, Luke dared not breathe. With one sharp movement Eddie sliced the club through the air landing in the long grass with a crack. Again and again he hammered the steel blade on the ground sending dirt and grass flying all around. He stopped and scanned the battered ground. Nothing. Eddie retreated removing a cloth from the bag and cleaning the mud from the club head. He got back into the buggy with de Vere while Luke gazed into the undergrowth.

"You'll have to drop a ball and lose a shot," instructed de Vere with glee.

Luke took a ball from the bag and dropped it on the edge of the rough. He hacked it out onto the fairway

"Probably never was a snake," derided de Vere to Eddie ensuring Luke heard as they drove away.

But Luke knew there was a snake, a dangerous snake.

They stood on the 17th, Luke had dropped a shot, he was now 1 behind with 2 to play, things did not look good and the snake was praying on his mind. DeVere teed off followed by Luke, two good shots in the middle of the fairway. They made their way down by the side on the lake, Luke looked at the bright sunlight shimmering on the water as it gently lapped the shore. He arrived at his ball, he needed a good shot. Addressing the ball he looked up at the flag in the distance. He swept the club through the air and watched the ball fly through the air. The direction was good, Luke let out a deep sigh of relief as it landed on the green.

"Give me the 9 iron," commanded De Vere.

"An 8 would be better from here," advised Eddie.

"I said the 9!"

Eddie quietly and obediently handed him the 9 iron. De Vere moved to the ball. The club swung violently hooking the ball over the lake and disappearing below the water with a plop. He glared angrily at Eddie, who remained silent looking at the sky, before turning his steely eyes on Luke. Luke looked at him sympathetically while trying to supress his joy.

De Vere strode to the water's edge, his face contorted and red with ire. He let out a yell, gripped the club by both ends and snapped it in two over his knee before tossing the parts out into the lake.

"You'll need to drop a ball and lose a shot," advised Luke calmly, quoting de Vere's words back to himself.

"I know what to do," growled de Vere. "Give me the 8 iron!"

He dropped a new ball and lashed his shot before storming back into the buggy and driving erratically away. Luke glanced back into the lake and smiled as he turned away. Behind him the snake raised its head as it glided through the water.

Despite de Vere losing his ball as they approached the last hole the scores were level. Luke walked pensively towards the final tee off area. His whole job depended on the next 150 yards. He looked down the lush green fairway to the flag gently fluttering in the breeze in the distance.

"Your turn," barked de Vere.

Luke removed an iron from his bag and carefully inspected the blade. He unzipped a side pocket and took out a small brush. Vigorously he rubbed the grooves on the club head, just one good shot he thought, almost praying. He put the brush back and rezipped the pocket before walking assuredly and placing his ball on the ground. Addressing the ball with the club positioned behind he observed the flag. He lowered his head and focused on the ball, flexing the club back, once , twice, he raised it high over his head. Suddenly, he stopped dead as he saw a buggy approaching out of the corner of his eye. It rumbled towards the group as Luke gently lowered his club.

"I thought I'd come for the big finish," boomed the boss stopping the buggy. "What's the score?"

"Level," replied De Vere.

"Level? So, it's all on the last hole. I like to see how a man reacts under real pressure. What greater pressure could there be than losing your source of income?"

Luke looked at the malevolent sparkle in his eyes as he puffed on a thick cigar.

"Well, get on with it Grainger," ordered the boss.

Luke moved back to his ball. He concentrated once again, positioning the club behind it, looking up and studying the flag position, focusing on the white ball, one more look at the flag, and lifting the club high. The blade sliced through the air, ripping across the top of the ground sending a small divot flying forwards as the ball soared high in the clear blue sky. It sailed through the radiant sun before landing on the green and stopping.

"Very nice shot, young Grainger," commended the boss.

De Vere turned to Eddie, Luke could see the tension in his face, he knew his shot was good.

"7," advised Eddie pulling the iron from the bag.

De Vere took the club silently and placed his ball on the ground. He took up his stance and swept the ball down the fairway.

"Great shot!" praised Eddie. "I think you're nearer the flag."

"Get in Grainger, I'll drive you down," said the boss.

Luke put his bag in the back of the buggy and they set off. As they got closer he could see the two balls on the green. His heart sank, de Vere had made a good shot, 4 feet from the flag, very puttable. His own was about 12 feet, things looked ominous. His mind turned once again to Caroline and their baby. How could he tell her he no longer had a job? He could get another, but when? The buggy stopped and they got out. Luke removed his putter from the bag and moved towards his ball. Placing his marker on the ground he picked it up and polished it with a cloth, all the time concentrating on the hole. 12 feet. His whole future depended on 12 feet. He replaced the ball and crouched down behind it looking at the line to the hole. A slight slope to the right. 12 feet. The most important 12 feet of his life. He stood up and placed the putter behind the ball. The boss, de Vere and Eddie looked on quietly. Luke was aware of the absolute stillness and silence that surrounded him. 12 feet. He slowly moved the putter back and glided it steadily forward. The ball rolled slowly towards the hole, the line looked good. Closer and closer it went. Luke held his breath, his heart beating fast. The ball caught the lip of the hole, circled it and trickled off to the side. Luke closed his eyes as his head drooped, the feeling of devastation sweeping through his entire body.

De Vere grinned and confidently removed his putter from his bag on the back of the buggy. He slowly and deliberately took the head cover off. Luke still had some faint hope, de Vere had to make the putt, albeit an easier one. De Vere placed his putter behind the ball. Luke observed him then the hole. De Vere was going to putt this, he was going to be fired, Luke knew it. As he looked at the grass he suddenly became aware of a faint zigzag trail leading to the hole. What was that? He heard the tap as de Vere's club made contact with the ball. It rolled gently towards the hole, straight and true, it was over. The ball trickled on, getting ever closer to the flag as Luke's heart sank. Just one more inch. The ball stopped. It sat on the very edge of the hole. No-one spoke. DeVere gritted his teeth and returned to the back of the buggy.

"We play an extra hole then," said Eddie.

The men looked at the ball sitting on the lip. Suddenly, there was a huge crash behind them. They turned to see De Vere standing beside his bag which was laying on the ground. Some of the clubs had come out with the impact.

"It's in!" cheered de Vere.

Luke turned back to the hole, de Vere's ball was gone.

"The vibration must have caused it to drop," said Eddie.

"That's blatant cheating," vented Luke.

"Very well played, Simon," congratulated the boss beaming.

"You can't do that," protested Luke. "That's totally against the rules."

"All is fair in love and war young Grainger. In business and golf too, you will learn."

Luke looked at the hole in disbelief as de Vere passed him grinning superciliously. Once again he observed the zigzag trail on the ground going towards the hole. Could it be? He watched silently as de Vere bent down and extended his hand forwards. Luke gritted his teeth and hardened his eyes. De Vere put his hand into the hole.

"I think I'll have this ball mounted on a solid gold plinth," he rejoiced holding it aloft.

Luke felt guilty, had he really wanted de Vere dead?

"Clear your desk this afternoon," ordered the boss.

Luke despondently lowered his head as he dawdled towards his ball passing a maliciously smiling de Vere. He bent down and picked it up.

"That's the sort of genius we need, Simon," enthused the boss patting him heartily on the back.

De Vere knelt in front of his bag and gripped the handle. Suddenly, he let out a blood curdling cry, recoiling and clutching his arm. All heads turned towards him. Looking down with an agonised expression on his face he saw the two small punctures and the blood seeping along his wrist. He staggered back as the triangular head emerged from inside the bag. His mind clouded and he collapsed on the ground. The group rushed towards him. They stopped abruptly as the snake raised his head hissing and bearing its deadly white mouth and fangs.

"Stay back!" shouted Eddie. "It's a Cottonmouth."

The snake slipped from the bag and slithered across the green.

"Call an ambulance!"

Luke watched as the yellow rings disappeared into the undergrowth.

Before the ambulance could arrive De Vere was dead.

TWIST IN THE TALE SHORT STORIES

TWIST IN THE TALE SHORT STORIES

The car skidded wildly across the ice, the tyres squealing as the driver hammered frantically on the foot brake in vain, leaving the road and hurtling into the tree with a terrifying crash.

"What the hell was that?"

He pushed his body up on the desk, above the semi-clad woman, her black blouse undone to expose her red satin bra and tight cleavage. He strained his eyes around the softly lit office.

"Just leave it William, she purred seductively, stretching her arms up to his shoulders and attempting to pull him back down.

"It came from outside."

He got up and made his way through the near darkness to the window while she sat up disgruntled on the desk and lit a cigarette. A street lamp partially illuminated the wreckage.

"Oh, my God!."

He went to the desk and lifted the phone.

"Which service do you require?"

"Ambulance."

The woman stood up and brushed down the skirt rucked up around her waist.

"There's been a car crash, the location is Redmond International Imports, the old Jefferson Industrial Estate. I can't see if anyone is hurt, but it looks bad,"

He put the phone down, buttoning up his shirt and tucking it into his trousers as he turned on the main light.

141

"The ambulance will be here soon."

The woman moved across the room and looked down at the mangled vehicle, in the distance she could hear the faint sound of sirens.

"The whole front is caved in, he must be dead."

The sirens became louder as the flashing blue lights approached at speed.

"I'd better go down," he said slipping on his jacket.

"I'll come with you".

"No, you stay here out of sight Angie, there are bound to be police, we can do without explaining your presence."

She nodded.

"Turn off the light so I can watch from the window."

He walked quickly down the stairs and out into the forecourt, tightening his jacket against the cold as the vehicles pulled up. Two paramedics moved rapidly to the crashed car and wrenched the buckled door open.

"She's still breathing."

"Ok. Let's get her out."

They removed the bloodied body from the wreckage, the airbag hanging loosely through the open door.

A uniformed constable advanced.

"Did you see the crash, sir?"

"No, I heard it from the office."

"I thought the buildings were derelict?"

"There are still a couple of businesses operating."

"I see, and what is your name?"

"William McCloud."

"Is anybody else in the building?"

"No," he replied running his hand through his wavy blonde hair. "I'm always first in and last out, Mr. Redmond likes it that way."

"Why are there two cars parked?"

William looked at the two vehicles side by side in front of the building entrance.

"The white Porsche belongs to Mr. Redmond. He leaves it here sometimes if he has a meeting in the city."

The ambulance pulled out and accelerated away with its lights flashing and sirens shrieking. The young officer scanned the scene, examining the ground.

"It seems she lost control on the ice, dangerous bend here."

He inspected the vehicle, crouching down at the side and lifting the deflated airbag.

"This has probably saved her life."

He placed it inside the vehicle and looked at the packages on the seats.

"Looks like she was a delivery driver/"

"Will that be all, officer?"

"We'll contact you if we need anything else, sir."

William returned to the office. Angie was still at the window.

"Was he dead?"

"She, it was a woman. No, it looks like she was saved by the airbag."

They watched as the police departed. Angie picked up a framed photograph of a chubby-faced, middle-aged man holding a cigar in one hand, a brandy in the other and smiling smugly.

"Damn I'm going to be late," she complained grabbing her coat and bag. " I wish it was him wrapped around a tree."

"Patience, Angie, he can't have too long left, the amount he drinks and smokes. You go, I'll lock up."

She blew him a kiss from her ruby red lips and went down the stairs.

****

"Angie! Where have you been until now?

She moved down the hall and into the lounge. A plump man was slumped in the plush, velvet armchair next to the roaring fire, a crystal glass hanging loosely from his hand and a half empty whisky bottle on the adjacent table. A cigar smouldered in the ashtray. He looked at her through his bleary eyes as she took off her fur-lined gloves and warmed her hands on the flames.

"Well?"

"I told you I was visiting Aunt Mary today."

"Until now?" he said looking down at his solid gold Rolex.

"She's not very well, you know that Phillip"

"Nothing trivial I hope."

She looked at him with disdain as he buried his fat face in the glass.

"And another thing, I told you not to take the Porsche."

"It works fine."

"The airbag light keeps coming on, it indicates it isn't working."

"Then get it fixed, darling. I've had a long day, I think I'll go to bed."

He watched as she vanished through the door and refilled his glass.

****

Phillip swivelled in his black, leather chair, phone pressed against his cheek and looked at the clear blue winter sky.

"Listen, Syed, I'm offering you 100 Taka per t-shirt, 10.000 units, do we have a deal?"

"I give you very best quality, I must ask 200 Taka."

"You forget I still have those documents, Syed. How old are those girls in your factory? It would be a great pity if it fell into the hands of the police in Dhaka."

145

"The British police would be interested in your involvement too."

"But I won't be doing 20 years in a Bangladeshi prison."

"Very well, 100 Taka."

"Cash on delivery."

He put the phone down, lit a thick cigar and studied the documents before placing them into a red folder.

"Willie!"

"You know I hate you calling me that."

He smiled smugly and puffed a ring of smoke up to the ceiling.

"The deal is on."

"Did he accept our price?"

"He did after a little persuasion," he said patting the red folder. "100 Taka per unit, what's that in pounds?"

"At the current exchange rate, 84p."

"We should be able to sell them on for £5 a unit."

He reached across the desk for his calculator.

"Let's see, £5 minus 84p, times 10,000, hmmm."

"£41,600."

Phillip beamed and smacked his chubby hands together.

"Not bad for a week's work, Willie."

146

William looked at the red folder.

"You should get rid of those documents, my name is on them."

"Are you afraid of playing hard ball?/"

"You will be incriminated as well as me."

"Relax Willie, we are perfectly safe. I'll keep it at home, put it in the Porsche after you have taken it to the garage."

"The garage?"

"Yes, the airbag light is still coming on. Bloody thing, you pay £100, 000 for a top of the range sports car and within a year it develops a fault. Don't let them charge you, bunch of thieving cowboys. After that arrange the delivery and despatch of the new merchandise. I'm having lunch in the city, could be another deal, where is Uzbekistan? Never mind, not important, the only thing that matters is the price."

He held out the key on the end of his extended finger. William walked slowly around the desk and took it.

"Drop it off at the house when you finish tonight, I want to come in early tomorrow morning."

He smirked as the door opened.

"Angie! What are you doing here?"

"I thought you were taking me to lunch."

"Not today, I've got an important business meeting," he said dismissively putting on his jacket.

"You promised!"

He strode past her and stopped at the top of the stairs.

"Willie, get her a Big Mac."

She scowled as he disappeared.

"And don't forget about the car!."

They stood in silence and listened to his footsteps echoing in the stairwell before moving to the window and watching him get into a waiting taxi. She lit a cigarette.

"Pig! He's only getting a taxi so he can drink. Hopefully, he will drink himself to death."

She sucked hard on the cigarette.

"What did he mean about the car?"

"He wants me to take it to the garage."

"Why do you let him treat you like a dogsbody? You practically run this place."

"I will one day."

"It could be today. I could leave him, get a divorce, get half the money."

"With your past history? You'd be lucky to get a tenth."

"Is it my fault I like young men."

"Maybe something could be arranged."

"It had better be soon. If he was out of the way, you could have the business and I could have everything else, the house, the cars, the money."

William sat on the soft, cream, leather seat and admired the wood trim below the dashboard. He flipped up the cover and pressed the ignition button. The engine roared into life. He pulsed the accelerator feeling the power as his eyes caught the red warning light on the console, a seated man behind a circle. His brow furrowed as he stared at it, before looking up at the tree, the remains of the crashed car now taken away. The light disappeared as he turned off the engine. He got out and walked slowly over to the tree, studying the black tyre marks on the road and shuffling his feet on the tarmac, the ice had melted.

He returned, put his tool box into the Porsche and headed further into the industrial complex. He turned into a narrow strip of unoccupied units and stopped. With the engine off he released the bonnet. He selected a screwdriver and carefully opened the back of the dashboard. In the distance he could hear voices. He stopped and looked up furtively. Doors were slamming then an engine sounded. He listened as it got fainter and fainter.. Burying his head below the bonnet he worked feverishly.

Ten minutes later he had finished. In his fingers he held up a small bulb. He placed it into his pocket. The moment of truth, he pressed the ignition switch, the engine came immediately to life, the warning light was gone.

William looked through the office window at the black sky. The stars twinkled, he bit his lip. Would it rain over night? Would it be cold enough in the morning? He picked up the red folder, switched off the lights and locked the door. Outside he felt the icy cold on his face, tossed the folder into the boot of the Porsche and sped away.

He pulled into the gravel drive and stopped in front of the mansion. The lights in the porch illuminated the extensive gardens. He climbed the steps and rang the bell admiring the white marble pillars on either side of the large oak doors. Presently, he heard advancing footsteps in the hall. Angie opened the door.

"That's the car done, here's the key."

"He's not back yet, I don't think I can wait another day."

"Patience," he said kissing her soft, cherry lips. "Things are about to go our way."

Early the following morning William stood outside his house examining the ground, dry. He went into the garage and came out carrying two buckets.

At the office block he parked and walked quickly over to the tree, the ground was frosty but no ice. Anxiously, he looked at his watch, 6am, there was still time, the estate was quiet, it was unlikely anyone else would come in on a Sunday. It was a chance he would have to take. He returned to his car, took out the buckets and went into the building. When he re-emerged the buckets were full of water. He walked quickly over to the bend and soaked the tarmac, watching as the water spread out evenly along the road.

In the office he sat by the window and waited. Time went by so slowly, one hour, two hours, he glanced nervously at his watch, where was he?

Suddenly his mobile phone rang.

"I've done it."

"Angie?"

"He never came back last night, I've left him."

"Where are you/?"

"I'm just coming into the estate, I took the Porsche."

He looked through the window just as it raced onto the bend. It skidded violently across the ice, tyres screeching. On the phone he heard the high-pitched scream as he watched in horror. The Porsche careered off the road and slammed ferociously into the tree. The phone went dead, the only sound was the constant horn outside. He looked at the smoke drifting from the bonnet and the raised boot. The phone slipped from his fingers, smashing on the floor. In the distance he saw the blue flashing lights. He just stood aghast, looking at the mangled wreckage. He could see the black tyre marks on the tarmac. The police pulled up behind and a young officer stepped out. William watched as he approached the twisted, smouldering mess and looked inside. He shook his head at his colleague. As he walked tentatively across the ice he bent down and picked up something from the ground. William's face turned pale as he saw what he was holding. The red folder.

TWIST IN THE TALE SHORT STORIES

THE LAST

TRAIN

TWIST IN THE TALE SHORT STORIES

I was laying on my back with no recollection of where I was or how I had gotten here. Certainly, I was outside, I could feel the icy cold air on my face. Around me all was in darkness, pitch black darkness. I had never seen a night so dark, no moon or stars above, must be a heavy cloud cover but I could not even make that out. Below me I could feel small stones digging into my back and something cold and hard below my neck. I reached back and put my hand onto whatever it was. It was freezing, so cold my skin almost stuck to it. It was thicker than my hand and raised several inches from the ground. Some sort of metal, steel perhaps. I ran my hand along it but it was longer than my reach. Strange. I tentatively moved my leg and felt my shoe drag through the gravel until it was stopped by something hard. Tapping my foot against it I could feel its solidness. I sat up and ran my hand along it. Something wooden, a plank maybe. I knelt up and ran my hand along its length until I reached the metal object that had been under my neck. It couldn't be. I ran my hand back along it. No doubt about it. A steel rail. To confirm what I already knew I crawled beside the plank until I reached another steel rail parallel to the first. What was I doing laying on a railway track?

I sat dumbfounded and tried to think. My mind was blank. Had I been involved in an accident? I felt alright, no bones seemed to be broken and I was not in any pain. Where was I? Clearly on a railway line but apart from that I had no idea. Where was I going? Had I been on a train? I searched my pockets for some evidence, maybe a train ticket. Nothing. My pockets were empty. Where was my wallet, my keys? I never go out without my wallet and keys. Had I been robbed? Maybe I had been attacked and thrown on the track, left there for a train to slice my body in two. This thought sent a shiver down my spine. But I had no bruises or cuts. Perhaps I had been knocked

155

out with one swift blow. I felt the back of my head for a lump. Nothing. I just sat there in a state of bewilderment. Suddenly, I became conscious of the silence, the complete and utter silence. Surely, there would be some sound. Small animals moving about, the wind through the trees, distant car engines. Nothing. An eerie silence, not even another train. Another train? It would be perilous to linger, God knows how long I had already been here and I was getting colder. I ambled to my feet and made my way to the side of the track. There seemed to be a steep embankment, almost vertical and covered in some sort of slime. I crossed to the other side. A similarly slimy, vertical embankment. I would have to make my way along the railway line but which way? I looked to the left. Darkness. I looked to the right. Darkness. I had to choose a direction. For no good reason I walked to the right. I don't know that it would have made any difference if I had gone to the left.

I trudged along by the side of the track in the cold and the dark. No sign of life anywhere. Just groping in the dark hoping a train would not come along. The embankment was so close to the track could I avoid being hit? I had read about people lying between the two rails while the train thundered over the top of them. That would take a lot of courage. Could you be certain that your nerve would hold and be able to lay perfectly still? I increased my pace as much as I could, aware that I was completely blind in the darkness.

On and on I went, I don't know how long, 10 minutes, 20 minutes, I seemed to have no concept of time. Suddenly, I saw a dim light in the distance. I stopped abruptly, panic spread through my body. A train? I listened. Nothing. I focused on the light. It was still. I made my way carefully towards it. The light was faint but growing slowly brighter with each step I took. As I got closer I could see it was coming from the side of the track about 15 feet above it. My spirits were lifting, at last a glimmer of light in this pervasive, gloomy darkness. Perhaps some warmth also, so cold, so chillingly cold. Closer and closer I got to the light until I could see it illuminating a small area in a cone shape spreading down from above. It was some kind of lamp lighting up a raised level. A platform? Not much light for a platform. Perhaps there had been a power cut. As I got nearer and nearer I could just about make out the outline of something below the lamp. A figure? It was motionless. Whatever it was it was dark and thin, maybe 6 feet. Could it be? Another person? I felt a sudden rush of emotion. The sheer joy of finding another person in this dark, cold place. I quickly tempered my elation. Perhaps it was not another person, perhaps it was just a trick of the light making me see what I wanted so much to see. I kept moving forward, excited, apprehensive, my eyes focused solely on the figure. The outline becoming more and more vivid. The figure remained perfectly still. I was almost at the platform. It had to be a person. I could now see the outline of a robe with a hood covering the head. I was metres from the figure. The slimy embankment beside me was replaced by a hard brick wall about 4 feet high. I ran my hand along it as I continued towards the lamp, continually looking up at the motionless figure. Finally, I stopped below the lamp and the figure below. The hood was pulled completely over his head so I was unable to see his face. The robe was long and black and came down to the ground so no feet were visible. I expected him to look down at any moment. He would certainly help me up. Not a flicker of movement.

"Hello!, I called up."

Nothing. Had he heard me? He must have heard me

"HELLO!", I called louder. "Can you help me up?"

Nothing. Motionless like a statue.

I put both hands on the platform and began to clamber out, my feet trying to get some grip on the wall. Straining I managed to pull myself up until my body lay on the platform with my legs over-hanging. I dragged myself further onto the platform until my legs were up. For a moment I lay there recovering my energy. The figure beside me remained still. I scrambled to my knees and then to my feet. I looked at the stony still figure and then scanned around me. Perhaps he belonged to a religious order that had a vow of silence. That would not explain why he had not helped me off the track, perhaps he had taken a vow not to help his fellow man also. I gave a slight chuckle at my little joke. The figure turned his head towards me. I stopped chuckling abruptly and looked at him. Through the hood it seemed to be a black hole. Suddenly, it spoke.

"There has been an accident", it said slowly and deliberately in a gravelled voice.

"Oh", I replied hesitantly.

"On the track."

"Was it serious?"

"Someone was killed."

"That's very sad", I sympathised.

"It's the reason I'm here."

"Are you going to help?"

"In a way."

I didn't understand his cryptic answer but at least we were talking now.

"I was on the track myself", I said nervously.

"I know."

"I don't know how I got there."

I hoped he could provide an answer. I paused waiting for him to speak.

Silence.

I looked around me. The light only illuminated a small part of the platform. I could see nothing around it, just a platform and a single lamp in the middle of nowhere. I wondered where I was. I scanned for a sign. Nothing. Surely this station had a name. What was this place? I looked down. For the first time I became aware there was only a single track. I looked through the darkness across the track to the other side. It was hard to see but I don't think there was a platform opposite. A shudder went through my body, this was a strange place. Only one track, one platform and no name.

"There's only one platform", I said cautiously.

"Everyone gets on at this side", he replied.

"What about the people going in the other direction?"

"Everyone is going the same way."

A chill went through my body turning me to ice. In the distance I heard a faint rumbling cutting through the deathly silence. I looked down the track in the direction of the sound, the rumbling getting louder and louder. Then I saw the flaming smoke above the approaching train. I felt no elation, only acceptance.

"Is this my train?" I asked weakly.

"This is the last train."

An accident on the track, a station with no name, only one platform, everyone goes in the same direction.

The train was all in darkness as it pulled alongside the platform. The figure stepped forward slowly and steadily, gripping the handle with his bony hand and opening the door.

"I'll show you the way."

For a moment I stood still and looked at the train, smoke bellowing all around it. I moved forward and stepped inside. The figure entered behind me and closed the door.

TRENCH WARFARE

Tommy sheltered in a dark, damp corner of the trench. The explosions and accompanying gun fire were deafening and seemingly endless. The sky was temporarily lit up as each shell landed. Chaos reigned supreme as all around him his comrades returned fire, shooting blindly in the dark at an unseen enemy. Some men were shouting, psyching themselves up in the frenzy. Others were quiet, crouching down, occasionally raising their heads above the parapet and firing a few aimless shots before hurriedly cowering again. From time to time a gust of wind would blow smoke through the trench bringing with it the rancid smell of death. Beside him Tommy heard the thump as yet another body hit the ground. He looked down at the lifeless body and the red blood slowly seeping out from under the helmet forming a small pool in the mud. The sergeant yelled, whipping up those still alive. Tommy could just about make out his silhouette. Then he heard him groan and slump to the ground. He just lay there moaning. It's worse when they are badly injured .they just lay helplessly in the cold, wet muck waiting to die. Some scream in agony praying to live while they wait for the inevitable end, sights and sounds that will haunt Tommy for the rest his life. His freezing hands tightened on his rifle until his knuckles were white. He was being driven insane by the surrounding screams and explosions, a never-ending nightmare. He closed his eyes tight, how he wished he was back home in Blighty.

Across the barren wasteland Jurgen peered out over the parapet, his body against the trench wall and his rifle pressed against his cheek holding it securely, his finger hovering above the trigger. His comrade's head suddenly appeared beside him fired a few shots and quickly crouched back down. Jurgen remained statuesque, seemingly unruffled by the mayhem around him. No point wasting ammunition, he would fire when he had a target. He had lost count of the number he had killed, 30, 40, who knows. But he knew when they had been hit. Some just falling silently to the ground, others staggering and screaming. Sometimes he would hear them laying helplessly, groaning until he could hear them no more.

Tommy trembled, would his short life end in this frozen tundra. His thoughts turned to England and happier times. His life had been great, loads of mates and the girls loved him with his boyish good-looks and sharp dress. He could charm a girl onto her back and then move on to the next one. If they were upset and crying that wasn't his problem, they shouldn't drop their knickers so easily. A swift slap would soon put an end to their tears. That one girl got pregnant but a bit of persuasion and a back-street abortion fixed that. Besides he never saw her after that, in fact, no-one had. He briefly wondered what had happened to her but there was always another girl with loose knickers.

Jurgen looked down the barrel closing his left eye. He gently lifted the rifle and fired. In the distance he heard the groan and watched the figure fall to the ground. He felt neither joy nor sadness. He had been killing for so long now he had become numb to any feelings. They were the enemy, he had to do his job, fight for his country, protect his people. The only people he wanted to protect were his family, his wife and young daughter, waiting for him back home in Berlin. He hunched down in the trench and placed his rifle against the wall. Reaching into his breast pocket he removed a crumpled black and white photograph. He carefully smoothed it out. A warm summer's day in the park with clear blue sky above and lush green grass below. Sitting on a tartan blanket with his arm around Ingrid and Anna on his lap with her small arms around his neck all smiling with the sun on their faces. For an instant it made him smile, a brief moment of joy in this dismal barren wilderness. He carefully folded the photograph and placed it securely back inside his jacket pocket.

"CHARGE!"

Tommy's blood froze in his veins, the word he dreaded most bellowed in his ears, exploding inside his mind. His whole body seemed to slump as the rifle hung loosely in his hands.

"CHARGE!"

The command rang out again followed by accompanying battle cries as men on either side of him scrambled up the broken ladders out of the trench. Tommy's heart was beating fast as he tightened his grip on his gun. He unleashed a blood-curdling scream and frantically scrambled up the ladder, firing erratically as he ran through the smoke. His boots sunk into the wet mud with each step spraying cold muck up his trousers.

Jurgen lined up alongside his comrades, men he had not known a year ago but who were now, at this moment, the most important people in his life. He could barely hear the captain's orders above the explosions and gun fire. It didn't matter that the words were inaudible, he knew what he had to do. He fixed his steely gaze on the ladder against the trench wall and tightened his grip on his weapon prepared to do his duty. Around him his colleagues started shouting. Jurgen remained silent, for a fleeting moment the image of his wife and daughter came into his mind again. Pushing little Anna on the swing while Ingrid looked on. Then the image was gone. He moved purposely forward, gripping the ladder assuredly and ascending into the smoke. Outside of the sanctuary of the trench the noise was even more intense. High above him the sky was lit up with hues of orange and yellow shimmering through the dusky haze. He advanced scanning alertly all around him, his rifle pointing forward and his finger tensed on the trigger.

Tommy stopped running as thick smoke shrouded him. He stood still, in the distance he could hear sporadic shots and faint voices but could see none of his comrades. The explosions had ceased and he was conscious of being alone. The smoke began to dissipate and he could just about make out the outline of a figure ahead of him. He made his way forward with his gun at the ready. The figure was moving slowly towards him. Tommy strained his eyes as he peered through the smoke. Suddenly, the figure was statuesque before him causing Tommy to stop abruptly. He felt the cold wind blowing the smoke across his face and into the wilderness until all was clear. Tommy and Jurgen looked at each other. They were so close Tommy could see Jurgen's blue eyes. In that desolate place two figures stood face to face. They had never met, they knew nothing about each other, fate had thrust them together. Time stood still, a single shot rang out and a single body fell lifelessly to the ground.

OTHER BOOKS
BY A J BOOTHMAN

TWIST IN THE TALE SHORT STORIES VOLUME 2

Eight short stories of tension and suspense with surprising and unexpected endings

Spider

Kitty

Voodoo

Whatever It Takes

The Camp

Lorry

Magic

Haunted

THE RAVEN'S VENGEANCE

The first Teagan O'Riordan mystery.

Events from the past spawn great vengeance in the sleepy Irish village of Rathkilleen. To catch a killer Detective Teagan O'Riordan will have to discover the secret of the Raven.

A complex mystery thriller that embraces Irish culture and reaches across Africa.

TEAGAN AND THE ANGEL OF DEATH

The second Teagan O'Riordan mystery.

Devil worshippers bring sacrilege and death to Rathkilleen. Teagan has to unravel satanic rituals and demonic symbols in order to unmask the Angel of Death.

An intricate mystery thriller which extends across Europe.

SHEER HATE

The Vigil is a vicious online newspaper that revels in muckraking and delights in ruining lives, leaving a trail of victims in its wake with deadly consequences. Seductive reporter, Silky Stevens, and sleazy photographer, Frank Ebdon, will do anything to get a front-page story. Journalist, Nick Rose, struggles with his past, but is forced to use all his investigative skills to unmask a killer driven by sheer hate.

THE RIPPER CLUB

A grisly murder sets computer hacker, Chris, and psychology student, Emma, on the trail of a serial killer and the discovery of the mysterious Ripper Club. Their investigations take them back to Whitechapel 1888 and Jack the Ripper. As the story unfolds and the suspense builds, the connections between the past and the present are revealed. Can they identify the killer before it is too late?

JACKPOT MILLIONAIRE

Danny Taylor is a middle-aged, working-class bloke who dreams of a better life away from the drudgery of work and his mundane, repetitive existence. He fantasises about being rich and having fast cars and even faster women. All this could become a reality if only he could win the lottery. Would this really lead to the fantastic life he imagines?

Jackpot Millionaire is a hilarious, fast paced comedy.

Printed in Great Britain
by Amazon

42207051R00098

Restless Legs Syn<

A Beginner's Quick Start Guide for
RLS Through Diet and Other Home Remedies, With
Sample Recipes

2

Disclaimer

By reading this disclaimer, you are accepting the terms of the disclaimer in full. If you disagree with this disclaimer, please do not read the guide.

All of the content within this guide is provided for informational and educational purposes only, and should not be accepted as independent medical or other professional advice. The author is not a doctor, physician, nurse, mental health provider, or registered nutritionist/dietician. Therefore, using and reading this guide does not establish any form of a physician-patient relationship.

Always consult with a physician or another qualified health provider with any issues or questions you might have regarding any sort of medical condition. Do not ever disregard any qualified professional medical advice or delay seeking that advice because of anything you have read in this guide. The information in this guide is not intended to be any sort of medical advice and should not be used in lieu of any medical advice by a licensed and qualified medical professional.

The information in this guide has been compiled from a variety of known sources. However, the author cannot attest to or guarantee the accuracy of each source and thus should not be held liable for any errors or omissions.

You acknowledge that the publisher of this guide will not be held liable for any loss or damage of any kind incurred as a result of this guide or the reliance on any information provided within this guide. You acknowledge and agree that you assume all risk and responsibility for any action you undertake in response to the information in this guide.

Using this guide does not guarantee any particular result (e.g., weight loss or a cure). By reading this guide, you acknowledge that there are no guarantees to any specific outcome or results you can expect.

All product names, diet plans, or names used in this guide are for identification purposes only and are the property of their respective owners. The use of these names does not imply endorsement. All other trademarks cited herein are the property of their respective owners.

Where applicable, this guide is not intended to be a substitute for the original work of this diet plan and is, at most, a supplement to the original work for this diet plan and never a direct substitute. This guide is a personal expression of the facts of that diet plan.

Where applicable, persons shown in the cover images are stock photography models and the publisher has obtained the rights to use the images through license agreements with third-party stock image companies.

TABLE OF CONTENTS

Introduction

Restless legs syndrome (RLS), also known as Willis-Ekbom disease is a condition that can make an individual feel uncomfortable in his or her legs. The condition may cause an irresistible urge to move around, which can temporarily improve the discomfort.

RLS may start at any age, but it tends to worsen with age. Women are more likely to experience restless legs syndrome than men, and the condition may run in families.

Symptoms of RLS can include difficulty sleeping, which can lead to problems with concentration and fatigue. There are some simple things that people with restless legs syndrome can do to help relieve their symptoms, such as stretching and taking breaks often if they work at a desk all day.

Additionally, some medications can help treat RLS. However, side effects are possible with any medication, so it's important to talk to a doctor before starting any new treatment.

There is no cure for restless legs syndrome, but lifestyle changes and home remedies may help relieve symptoms.

In this beginner's guide, we'll discuss the following subtopics in detail:

• What causes restless legs syndrome?

• What are the symptoms of restless legs syndrome?

• Who is at risk to get restless legs syndrome?

• Why restless legs syndrome is more common in women than in men?

• How is restless legs syndrome diagnosed?

• What are the complications of restless legs syndrome?

• How is restless legs syndrome treated?

• What are the home remedies for restless legs syndrome?

• Managing restless legs syndrome through lifestyle changes.

• How to manage restless legs syndrome through diet?

So, if you or someone you know might have restless legs syndrome, read on to learn more about this condition and how to find relief.

What Causes Restless Legs Syndrome?

The exact cause of RLS is unknown, but it is thought to be related to abnormalities in the dopamine system. Several possible factors may also contribute to its development. These include genetics, age, vitamin deficiencies, pregnancy, diabetes, kidney failure, and Parkinson's disease. Additionally, lifestyle factors such as smoking and caffeine consumption can also increase a person's risk of developing RLS.

Age and Genes: RLS can occur at any age, but it is most common in middle-aged and elderly adults. In some cases, RLS is a genetic disorder, which means that it runs in families. Up to 92% of patients with RLS have a first-degree relative with the disorder. These patients tend to develop symptoms earlier in life (before age 45) than those without the genetic link.

Vitamin deficiencies: Vitamins play an important role in nerve function, and deficiencies can lead to all sorts of problems. Vitamin D is essential for calcium absorption, and it also plays a role in nervous system function. A lack of vitamin D has been linked to an increased risk of restless legs syndrome.

Vitamin B12 is another important nutrient for nerve function. A deficiency in vitamin B12 can cause nerve damage, which may lead to the development of restless legs syndrome. Iron is also vital for healthy nerve function. An iron deficiency can cause symptoms like fatigue and weakness, which can contribute to the development of restless legs syndrome.

Iron deficiency: Iron deficiency is one of the most common risk factors. Iron plays a key role in the production of dopamine, a neurotransmitter that helps to regulate movement. When iron levels are low, dopamine production can be impaired, leading to symptoms of RLS.

Pregnancy: Pregnancy is a common trigger for restless legs syndrome. This may be due to the hormonal changes that occur during pregnancy, which can affect the nervous system. Additionally, pregnancy can lead to iron deficiency, which has been linked to RLS.

Diabetes: One of the less well-known complications of diabetes is restless legs syndrome (RLS). Diabetes can cause changes in dopamine levels, leading to the characteristic symptoms of RLS.

Parkinson's disease: Parkinson's disease is a condition that also results in an imbalance of dopamine. Not surprisingly, Parkinson's disease is one of the most common causes of restless legs syndrome.

Kidney failure: While the exact cause of RLS is unknown, it is thought to be linked to an imbalance of certain chemicals in the brain, including dopamine and iron. Kidney failure can cause an imbalance of these chemicals, leading to the development of RLS.

Smoking: Cigarette smoke contains several harmful chemicals, including nicotine and carbon monoxide. These substances can damage the nerves and disrupt circulation, both of which are linked to RLS. In addition, smoking makes it more difficult for the body to absorb iron, and iron deficiency has been linked to RLS. If you smoke and have symptoms of RLS, quitting smoking may help to improve your condition. Talk to your doctor about ways to quit smoking and ease your RLS symptoms.

Caffeine consumption: Those who consume large amounts of caffeine are more likely to experience symptoms of restless legs syndrome. While the exact mechanism is not known, it is believed that caffeine interferes with the body's ability to regulate dopamine levels.

Dopamine is a neurotransmitter that plays a role in movement and coordination. When levels are off, it can lead to involuntary movements, such as the twitching or jerking associated with restless legs syndrome. Caffeine may also increase nerve activity, which can aggravate symptoms.

Overall, there are many potential causes of restless legs syndrome. If you think you may have RLS, talk to your doctor. He or she can help you identify the underlying cause and develop a treatment plan.

What Are the Symptoms of Restless Legs Syndrome?

The most common symptom of RLS is an overwhelming urge to move your legs, which can be accompanied by a tingling or burning sensation. Other symptoms include fatigue and insomnia.

An overwhelming urge to move your legs: This is the most characteristic symptom of RLS. You may feel an irresistible urge to move your legs, which can be accompanied by a tingling or burning sensation. The urge to move is often worse when you are lying down or sitting for long periods. You may feel restless and unable to keep still. This can make it difficult to fall asleep or stay asleep.

Fatigue: Fatigue is a common symptom of restless legs syndrome. You may find it difficult to concentrate during the day and may feel tired even after a full night's sleep. The cause of this fatigue is unknown, but it may be related to the inability to get a restful night's sleep. If you have restless legs syndrome, you may find yourself waking up multiple times during the night. This can lead to feelings of exhaustion during the day.

Insomnia: Insomnia is often a result of the other symptoms of RLS. The constant urge to move can make it difficult to fall asleep. Once you do fall asleep, you may be awakened by the sensation or by the need to move your legs. As a result, you may not get a full night's sleep and may feel tired during the day.

The symptoms of RLS can vary in severity. For some people, they are mild and only occur occasionally. For others, the symptoms can be severe and may interfere with daily activities.

Who is at risk to get restless legs syndrome?

As mentioned above, there are many potential risk factors for restless legs syndrome. Some of these are modifiable, which means they can be changed. For example, quitting smoking or cutting back on caffeine may help to reduce your symptoms. Other risk factors, such as age and family history, cannot be changed.

That said, there are some groups of people who are at an increased risk for developing RLS. These include:

Women: Women are more likely to develop RLS than men. This may be due to hormonal changes, such as those that occur during pregnancy.

Older adults: The risk of RLS increases with age. This may be due to the natural decline in dopamine levels that occurs with age.

People with a family history of RLS: If you have a family member with RLS, you may be more likely to develop the condition yourself. This suggests that there may be a genetic component to RLS.

People with certain medical conditions: Conditions that can cause changes in dopamine levels or iron levels, such as Parkinson's disease or diabetes, are linked to an increased risk of RLS.

If you have any of the above risk factors, talk to your doctor. He or she can help you monitor your symptoms and take steps to prevent RLS from developing.

Why Restless Legs Syndrome Is More Common in Women Than in Men?

Many people suffer from restless legs syndrome (RLS), a condition that causes an uncomfortable sensation in the legs and an irresistible urge to move them. However, RLS is more common in women than in men, and there are several possible explanations for this gender disparity.

Estrogen

Estrogen has long been known to influence dopamine activity in the brain, but its exact role in movement disorders like RLS and schizophrenia has been unclear. New research suggests that estrogen may play a significant role in these disorders, but it is the fluctuations in estrogen levels rather than the overall amount that is most influential.

This theory could help explain why RLS is more common in women than men, as women's estrogen levels fluctuate throughout their lives, particularly during pregnancy. This link provides a possible explanation for why pregnancy is often a trigger for RLS symptoms. While more research is needed to confirm this connection, the new findings could lead to improved treatments for RLS and other movement disorders.

Iron Deficiency

Iron is an essential mineral that plays a role in many different bodily functions. It helps to carry oxygen in the blood, supports a healthy immune system, and is necessary for cell growth. Iron is necessary for the proper function of dopamine, a neurotransmitter that helps to regulate movement.

However, iron can also be easily lost through bleeding, and during pregnancy, iron requirements increase as the volume of blood in the body increases. This can put pregnant women at risk for iron deficiency anemia. This is maybe why women are more likely to be iron-deficient than men. Iron deficiency can lead to several problems, including fatigue, lowered immunity, and impaired cognitive function. However, one of the most common symptoms of iron deficiency is restless legs syndrome (RLS).

Low levels of iron can disrupt dopamine signaling and lead to the involuntary movement characteristic of RLS. If you think you may be iron-deficient, talk to your doctor about getting a blood test. Treating iron deficiency can often help to relieve the symptoms of RLS.

Medications

Comorbidity, or the presence of more than one disease in an individual, is common in women and may act as a trigger for emerging restless legs syndrome (RLS). Women are more likely to suffer from migraines, sleep disorders, depression, and anxiety than men, and all of these diseases have potential treatments that could make RLS worse. For example, some drugs used to treat migraines can serve as RLS triggers.

A comorbid disease or its treatment may activate the neural pathways involved in RLS, explaining why more women suffer from this condition. There are a variety of other comorbid diseases and drug treatments that can potentially make RLS worse, making it important for clinicians to be aware of this potential when treating patients with comorbidities.

If you're a woman with RLS, talk to your doctor about the possibility that a comorbid disease or its treatment may be worsening your symptoms. There are often treatments available that can help to relieve RLS triggered by comorbidity.

How Is Restless Legs Syndrome Diagnosed?

There is no one test to diagnose RLS, but a diagnosis will be based on your symptoms, medical history, family history, physical examination, and test results. Your GP should be able to diagnose restless legs syndrome, but they may refer you to a neurologist if there is any uncertainty.

Physical examination and medical history: When trying to determine whether a person has restless legs syndrome, doctors will often look for certain key symptoms.

First, the person typically experiences an overwhelming urge to move their legs, often accompanied by an uncomfortable sensation such as itching or tingling.

Second, the symptoms usually occur or get worse when the person is resting or inactive.

Third, the symptoms are often relieved by moving the legs or stretching them.

Finally, the symptoms are typically worse during the evening or at night.

If a person experiences these symptoms regularly, they may be diagnosed with restless legs syndrome.

Assessment: GPs or specialists will ask about the pattern of your symptoms to help assess their severity. It is important to keep track of when your symptoms occur and how long they last. Additionally, you may be asked about any factors that seem to aggravate or relieve your symptoms. This information can help your doctor determine whether you have RLS and, if so, how best to treat it.

Blood test: Your GP may also refer you for blood tests to rule out underlying causes. Blood tests can help to assess conditions such as anemia, diabetes, and kidney function problems. It is particularly important to find out the levels of iron in your blood because low iron levels can sometimes cause secondary RLS.

Polysomnography test: If you have restless legs syndrome and it's disrupting your sleep, you may be referred to a sleep clinic. There, they may recommend a polysomnography test. This test measures your breathing rate, brain waves, and heartbeat throughout the night. The results of this test can help determine if you have periodic limb movements in sleep (PLMS).

Early diagnosis and treatment of restless legs syndrome are important to prevent the condition from becoming worse. If you think you may have RLS, see your GP for an assessment.

What Are the Complications of Restless Legs Syndrome?

Most people with RLS do not have any major problems. However, some people have severe symptoms which can cause emotional discomfort, disrupted sleep patterns, and daytime drowsiness. People with severe RLS might want to avoid activities that involve sitting down for long periods, such as going to the movies or driving for long distances. This is because the problem gets worse when they are resting.

Emotional discomfort: Many people with RLS feel anxious or depressed because of their condition. This may be because they are not getting enough sleep, or because they are worried about the potential consequences of their condition.

Sleep disruption: People with RLS often have difficulty falling asleep and staying asleep. This can lead to fatigue during the day and potentially reduce productivity at work or school.

Daytime drowsiness: Some people with RLS find that their symptoms cause them to feel very tired during the day. This can make it difficult to concentrate and make it more likely that they will have accidents.

If you have RLS, it is important to talk to your GP about your symptoms and how they are affecting your life. They can provide you with information and support to help you cope with the condition. Additionally, they can refer you to a sleep specialist if your condition is causing significant disruption to your sleep.

How Is Restless Legs Syndrome Treated?

The following medications are the ones that doctors recommend for treating restless legs syndrome: dopaminergic drugs, alpha-2-delta ligands, and opioids. These drugs can be taken alone or in combination with other medications. Your doctor will develop the best treatment plan for you based on the severity of your symptoms and your medical history.

Dopaminergic drugs: Dopaminergic drugs are a common treatment for RLS. These drugs work by increasing levels of dopamine in the brain, which helps to improve nerve function and relieve symptoms. Levodopa/carbidopa and ropinirole are two dopaminergic drugs that are commonly used to treat RLS.

Alpha-2-delta ligands: Alpha-2-delta ligands are a type of drug that is often used to relieve the symptoms of RLS. Gabapentin and pregabalin are two common examples of alpha-2-delta ligands, and they work by binding to a protein in the brain that is involved in transmitting nerve signals.

This action helps to reduce the abnormal activity in the nerves that are thought to be responsible for the symptoms of RLS. Alpha-2-delta ligands are typically well tolerated, but some side effects may occur.

Opioids: Opioids such as oxycodone work by blocking pain signals from the brain. They are typically used for short-term relief of RLS symptoms. However, there is a risk of addiction and other side effects with opioids, so they should be used with caution.

Anticonvulsants: Anticonvulsants are a type of medication commonly used to treat RLS. These drugs work by stabilizing nerve cell activity and reducing inflammation. One of the most commonly prescribed anticonvulsants for RLS is gabapentin. Other anticonvulsants that may be used to treat RLS include pregabalin, levetiracetam, and topiramate.

Iron supplements: RLS is often associated with iron deficiency, and treatment typically involves taking iron supplements. Iron is essential for the production of dopamine, which helps to regulate movement. Low levels of dopamine are thought to be responsible for the twitching and discomfort associated with RLS. In addition, iron supplements can help to improve the quality of sleep by reducing nighttime leg movements.

While these medications can be effective in relieving symptoms, they can also cause side effects such as drowsiness, dizziness, and nausea. It is important to discuss potential risks and benefits with a doctor before starting any treatment.

What Are the Home Remedies for Restless Legs Syndrome?

Although home remedies may not completely get rid of your RLS symptoms, they may help to minimize them. You may need to experiment with different combinations of treatments to find the cures that work best for you.

Massage: Massage can help to relax the muscles and reduce inflammation. It can also promote circulation and improve nerve function. For best results, massage the affected area for 10-15 minutes before bedtime. You can also try using essential oils, such as lavender or chamomile, to help relax the muscles.

Hot bath: Hot water will relax the muscles and ease the discomfort. To try this remedy, fill a bathtub with hot water and soak for 20 minutes. You may need to experiment with the temperature of the water to find what works best for you. Some people find that adding Epsom salt to the water can also help.

After soaking, dry off completely and apply a lotion or cream to your legs. This home remedy may not work for everyone, but it is worth a try if you are struggling with restless legs syndrome.

Hot/cold compress: Applying alternating periods of heat and cold to the affected area can help to reduce muscle tension and pain. For best results, start with a warm compress for three minutes, followed by a cold compress for one minute. Repeat this cycle three times. You can do this treatment as needed, but be sure to stop if you experience any pain or discomfort.

Physical therapy: By stretching and massaging the legs, physical therapy can help to reduce muscle tension and improve circulation. Additionally, physical therapy can help to strengthen the muscles, which may help to reduce the urge to move the legs. While there is no guarantee that physical therapy will eliminate all symptoms of restless legs syndrome, it may provide some relief and allow sufferers to get a better night's sleep.

It is crucial to keep in mind that the home remedies included here are not a cure for restless legs syndrome; nonetheless, they may be helpful in the management of your symptoms. If you are having trouble finding relief, you should discuss different treatment options with your primary care provider.

What Are the Lifestyle Changes that Can Help Treat Restless Legs Syndrome?

In addition to home remedies and medications, some lifestyle changes can also help to ease the symptoms of restless legs syndrome. These changes can include:

Exercise: Increased circulation and decreased muscular tension are two benefits that may be achieved through exercise. Because too much exercise might make RLS symptoms worse, you must select a method of physical activity that is effective for you. A schedule consisting of moderate activity, such as walking, is typically recommended.

Sleep: A sufficient amount of sleep is necessary for the management of RLS. The majority of adults require seven to eight hours of sleep every single night. If you are having difficulties falling or staying asleep, setting a schedule for when you go to bed may help.

Avoid consuming coffee and alcohol in the hours leading up to bedtime, and make your bedroom as peaceful as possible by turning down the lights and selecting bedding that is comfortable for you.

Stress management: The trigger of symptoms of restless legs syndrome (RLS) is frequently precipitated by emotional or physical stress. Your body will produce adrenaline and other chemicals in response to stress, both of which will cause an increase in your heart rate and blood pressure. This may result in emotions of worry, anxiety, and irritation in the individual. In addition, stress can disrupt sleep, which can make the symptoms of restless leg syndrome (RLS) worse.

There are several things that you may do to better manage your stress if you are currently experiencing difficulties in this area. Counseling, physical activity, and mental health practices like yoga and meditation are all proven methods for lowering stress levels.

Dietary changes: Some individuals report that eating particular foods might trigger RLS symptoms. If you want to experience fewer of these symptoms, avoiding the foods that trigger them is a good idea. Caffeine, alcohol, and nicotine are three common items that might set off an allergic trigger. Eating a diet that is balanced and avoiding foods that have been processed are both things that can help minimize discomfort.

Quit smoking: If you smoke, stopping the habit can help lower the severity of RLS symptoms. To make restless leg syndrome (RLS) symptoms even more severe, smoking reduces the quantity of oxygen that travels to the legs.

The illness known as restless legs syndrome is a long-term one that can be challenging to treat. You may be able to alleviate your symptoms and have a more restful night's sleep by turning to home remedies and making adjustments to your lifestyle. If you are having trouble finding relief, you should discuss different treatment options with your primary care provider.

Managing RLS Through Diet

Dietary changes could prove beneficial in the treatment of restless legs syndrome symptoms. There is some evidence that suggests that eating particular foods might trigger RLS symptoms in some people. If you want to experience fewer of these symptoms, avoiding the foods that trigger them may help.

Caffeine, alcohol, and nicotine are three of the most common things that can trigger RLS symptoms. Eating a healthy, well-balanced diet and avoiding items that have been processed can also help to lessen symptoms.

Caffeine: Caffeine is a stimulant that may be found in beverages like coffee and tea, as well as chocolate and energy drinks. Caffeine, even though it may seem like a harmless pick-me-up, can make the symptoms of restless legs syndrome worse.

Caffeine is known to interact with the neurological system, which can lead to irritability and make current symptoms even worse. In addition to this, coffee is known to disrupt sleep, which is something that must be prioritized while treating restless legs syndrome. If you suffer from restless legs syndrome, it is in your best interest to abstain from caffeine entirely or to restrict your consumption to very low levels.

Alcohol: People who suffer from restless legs syndrome (RLS) may discover that consuming alcohol makes their symptoms much more severe. This is not an unusual occurrence.

It is believed that alcohol may prevent the body from absorbing iron by interfering with the body's capacity to absorb iron. The specific mechanism behind this is not completely known. Lack of iron, which plays a crucial part in nerve function, has been linked to symptoms of restless legs syndrome (RLS).

In addition, alcohol can have a diuretic effect, leading to both dehydration and electrolyte imbalances, both of which can bring on symptoms of restless legs syndrome (RLS). Because of these factors, it is recommended that persons who have RLS cut back on their use of alcohol.

Nicotine: As a stimulant, nicotine has the potential to bring on or exacerbate symptoms of restless legs syndrome. Because it excites the nervous system and makes people move their legs more often, nicotine can make restless leg syndrome symptoms worse. A disturbed sleep pattern is another factor that can add to the discomfort of restless legs syndrome. Nicotine is known to cause sleep disruptions.

Putting an end to one's use of cigarettes and other tobacco products may help lessen the intensity of symptoms. Talk to your healthcare provider about drugs or other therapies that could be helpful if you're having trouble quitting smoking.

Excess Salt: Consuming foods that are heavy in salt can, according to the experiences of some people, bring on symptoms of restless legs syndrome. It is not obvious why this is the case, although it may have something to do with how salt influences the circulation of blood. For instance, consuming an excessive amount of salt can contribute to inflammation and the constriction of blood vessels, both of which can cause pain and cramping in the legs.

Whether you have a suspicion that salt is the cause of your restless legs syndrome symptoms, you might want to try reducing the number of salty foods you eat and seeing if this makes any difference in the severity of your symptoms.

Processed Foods: Processed foods tend to have a high concentration of fats and chemicals that aren't good for you, which might bring on symptoms of restless legs syndrome (RLS). Consuming processed foods can upset this delicate balance, which in turn might cause symptoms to become more severe. If you have restless legs syndrome (RLS), you should probably cut back on the number of processed foods you eat.

Refined Sugars: Many processed foods include refined sugars, which are known to be a potential cause of restless legs syndrome symptoms because of their ability to cause an imbalance in blood sugar levels.

In addition, processed carbohydrates can cause inflammation, which can make symptoms even worse. This can further complicate the situation. If you are sensitive to restless legs syndrome, it is essential to cut back on your consumption of refined sugar for the reasons given above.

Recommended dietary changes

Changing your diet in certain ways, in addition to avoiding the items that tend to set off your RLS symptoms, might help reduce their severity. These changes include the following:

Increasing iron intake: The condition that causes restless legs syndrome requires iron. RLS has been connected to iron deficiency, and research has shown that increasing one's iron consumption can assist to lower the severity of RLS symptoms. Beans, dark leafy greens, red meat, and cereals that have been fortified with iron are all excellent sources of iron.

Eating magnesium-rich foods: Magnesium is necessary for a wide variety of body activities, such as the contraction of muscles, the transmission of nerve impulses, and the generation of energy. Increasing the amount of magnesium in your diet could help to alleviate the symptoms of RLS. Dark chocolate, pumpkin seeds, spinach, and quinoa are all excellent food choices that are high in magnesium.

Increasing folate intake: Folate is a kind of vitamin B that is essential for those who have RLS. A lack of folate in the diet has been associated with restless legs syndrome (RLS), and there is evidence that increasing folate consumption might help lessen RLS symptoms. Foods like dark leafy greens, legumes, nuts, and cereals that have been fortified with folate are all good sources of folate.

Eating potassium-rich foods: One of the minerals that are necessary for the health and performance of one's muscles is potassium. It is essential for maintaining proper fluid balance in addition to assisting in the regulation of nerve impulses and muscle contractions. Increasing the amount of potassium that you consume may help to alleviate some of the symptoms of RLS. Bananas, sweet potatoes, avocados, and yogurt are all good examples of foods that are rich in potassium.

You can assist to lessen the intensity of your restless legs syndrome (RLS) symptoms by adhering to these dietary guidelines.

Sample Recipes

Baked Salmon

Ingredients:

- 2 salmon fillets

- 6 cups of fresh spinach

- 2 tsp. coconut oil

- 1/4 tsp. garlic powder

- 1/4 tsp. turmeric

- 3 large cloves of garlic

- lemon juice

- salt

- pepper

Instructions:

1. Preheat the oven to 400°F.

2. Line a baking dish with parchment paper.

3. Marinate salmon fillets in lemon juice, coconut oil, garlic powder, turmeric, salt, and pepper.

4. Let it sit for a few minutes. This may also be done the night before to help the juices and flavor get into the salmon.

5. Once the oven is ready, bake the salmon for 15 minutes.

6. Cook some of the garlic in a pan with coconut oil.

7. Add spinach and cook until ready. Season with salt and pepper to taste.

8. Take salmon out of the oven and put spinach beside it.

9. Serve and enjoy.

Grilled Macrobiotic Bowl with Stir Fry Broccoli, Onions, and Carrots

Ingredients

- 2 tbsp. garlic, minced

- 2 tbsp. olive oil

- 1/2 cup adzuki beans cooked

- 1/2 cup sauerkraut

- 1 cup quinoa

- 1/2 cup cubed butternut squash

- 1 tbsp. dulse flakes

- 1 1/2 cup baby kale

- 1 tbsp. toasted pumpkin seeds

- salt

- pepper

Garlic Cashew Creme:

- 3 cloves garlic

- 1/2 cup raw cashews

- 1 lemon, juice only

- 1/2 tsp. sea salt

Instructions:

1. Add the butternut to a large glass bowl to pre-cook for 2 minutes.

2. On the grill, spread some olive oil. Add rice, butternut, sauerkraut, greens, and beans.

3. For 5 to 7 minutes, grill on medium-high, turning the ingredients frequently until cooked.

4. Sprinkle a dash of salt and pepper to taste.

5. To make the garlic cashew creme, blend all ingredients in a high-speed blender; set aside.

6. Assemble the bowl by sprinkling dulse flakes and toasted pumpkin seeds and top with garlic cashew creme.

Arugula and Mushroom Salad

Ingredients:

- 5 oz. arugula washed

- 1 lb. fresh mushrooms

- 1/4 tsp. shoyu

- 1/2 red onion

- 1 tbsp. olive oil

- 1 tbsp. mirin

For tofu cheese:

- 1/8 cup umeboshi vinegar

- 1/2 firm tofu

Instructions:

1. In a bowl, add the rinsed tofu. Crumble and pour in vinegar.

2. In a separate bowl add shoyu, red onions, salt, olive oil, and mirin. 3. Mix to combine.

4. Add in the arugula and toss to combine with the dressing.

5. Serve and enjoy.

Asian Zucchini Salad

Ingredients:

- 1 medium zucchini, sliced thinly into spirals

- 1/3 cup rice vinegar

- 3/4 cup avocado oil

- 1 cup sunflower seeds, shells removed

- 1 lb. cabbage, shredded

- 1 tsp. stevia drops

- 1 cup almonds, sliced

Instructions:

1. Cut the zucchini spirals into smaller parts. Set aside.

2. Put almonds, sunflower seeds, and cabbage in a large bowl. Combine the ingredients well.

4. Add zucchini to the mixture.

5. In a small bowl, mix vinegar, stevia, and oil using a whisk or fork.

6. Pour vinegar mixture all over the zucchini mixture. Toss well. Make sure everything is covered with the dressing.

7. Refrigerate for 2 hours before serving.

Asparagus and Greens Salad with Tahini and Poppy Seed Dressing

Ingredients:

- 10 to 12 asparagus stalks, washed well and sliced into ribbons

- 5 radishes, washed well, and sliced thinly

- 2 to 3 rainbow carrots, peeled and sliced thinly

- 1 handful wild spinach

- 1 small handful of microgreens, washed well

- 1 small handful of sunflower greens, washed well

- optional: few pieces of chive blossoms

For the dressing:

- 2 tbsp. tahini

- 1 tbsp. poppy seeds

- 1 tbsp. extra-virgin olive oil

- salt

- pepper

Instructions:

1. For the dressing, whisk ingredients together in a small bowl.

2. In a separate bowl, toss salad ingredients in the mixture.

3. Drizzle dressing on salad upon serving.

Garbanzo-Kale and Butternut Squash Burger

Ingredients:

- 1/2 cup brown rice

- 1/2 cup quinoa

Beetroot burger:

- 2 cups kale, chopped

- 1 tsp. paprika

- 1 cup butternut squash, chopped

- 1/2 cup sauerkraut, bottled

- 3/4 cup garbanzo beans

- 2 tbsp. coconut oil

- 1 tsp. sea salt

Instructions:

1. In a pan, boil quinoa and water. Cook for 20 minutes. Set aside

2. Combine kale and butternut squash in a small bowl.

3. Add the paprika, garbanzo beans, sea salt, and coconut oil.

4. Sauté the mixture until vegetables soften.

5. Prepare the burger by making balls. Flatten the burger and fry until done.

6. Use quinoa and rice as buns for the burger.

Broccoli-Kale with Avocado Toppings Rice Bowl

Ingredients:

- 1/2 avocado
- 2 cups kale
- 1 cup broccoli florets
- 1/2 cup cooked brown rice
- 1 tsp. plum vinegar
- 2 tsp. tamari
- sea salt, to taste

Instructions:

1. In a small pot, simmer broccoli florets, and kale in about 3 tbsp. of water. Cook for 2 minutes.

2. Add tamari, vinegar, and cooked brown rice. Stir to combine.

3. Transfer pot contents into a medium-sized bowl and top with sliced avocado; sprinkle a dash of sea salt to taste.

4. Serve immediately.

Steak and Mushrooms

Ingredients:

- 4 T- bone beef steak

- 1/4 cup rice bran oil

- 600 grams of Asian mushrooms (e.g. Shiitake, Oyster, Swiss Brown, King Brown)

- 1 cup coriander

- 1 cup mint leaves

- 1/4 garlic chives

- 4 celery sticks

- 2 carrots, thinly sliced

- 200 grams of sugar snaps

- 1/4 red onion, thinly sliced

For the dressing:

- 1/4 cup soy sauce

- 1/4 cup mirin

- 2 tbsp. rice vinegar

- 1 long red chili, finely chopped

- 2 tsp. grated gingers

- 1 crushed garlic clove

Instructions:

Dressing:

1. Put the ingredients of the dressing altogether in a screw-cap glass jar.

2. Seal the jar and shake well to combine.

T-bone Steak:

1. Heat a barbecue or grilling pan.

2. Place the steaks over the grills.

3. Brush the steaks with oil. Season the meat with herbs, salt, and pepper.

4. For medium-rare, cook each side for about 6 minutes.

5. Place the mushrooms on the grilling pan, brush with oil, and allow to cook well.

6. Combine the cooked mushrooms with the prepared dressing sauce.

7. While waiting for the meat to cook, mix carrots, snaps, and red onion in a bowl to make a salad. Add some dressing.

8. Place the steak on a plate topped with mushrooms and garlic chives.

9. Serve with salad and the remaining dressing.

Steak with Olive Oil

Ingredients:

• 2 8-oz. grass-fed New York strip steaks, about 1-1/2-inch-thick, trimmed

• 3 tbsp. olive oil, divided

• 1 tsp. freshly ground black pepper, divided

• 1 tsp. kosher salt, divided

• 1 garlic clove, crushed

• 1 rosemary sprig

• optional: rosemary leaves

Instructions:

1. Place the grill pan over medium-high heat.

2. Brush a tablespoon of oil on the steak, then sprinkle with half a teaspoon of salt and another half teaspoon of pepper.

3. Put a tablespoon of oil into the pan, followed by a rosemary sprig and garlic.

4. Cook steak for about 9 minutes, or until preferred doneness is achieved. For every minute, turn the steak and baste it with oil.

5. Transfer the steak to a cutting board, letting it rest for 5 minutes.

6. Slice steak across the grain and place it on a platter. Drizzle with the juice from the cutting board and the leftover oil.

7. Sprinkle it with the remaining salt and pepper.

8. Upon serving, garnish with rosemary leaves if desired.

Summary

Restless legs syndrome, often known as RLS, is a prevalent condition that has the potential to have a considerable negative impact on one's quality of life. A neurological condition known as restless legs syndrome leads sufferers to have an uncontrolled need to move their legs, which is typically brought on by an unpleasant feeling in the legs.

Although the root cause of restless legs syndrome has not been pinpointed, researchers believe that it is connected to dysfunctions in the neural system. The involuntary impulse to move one's legs, an unpleasant feeling in one's legs, and an inability to fall or stay asleep are all indications of restless legs syndrome.

The condition known as restless legs syndrome strikes people of any age and is more frequent in women than in males. Typically, the diagnosis is reached by considering both the patient's symptoms and the results of any relevant testing. Although there is no cure for restless legs syndrome, there are several therapies that can help reduce the symptoms and make living with the condition more bearable.

A few of the more common home treatments for restless legs syndrome include avoiding coffee and alcohol, engaging in consistent physical activity, and taking dietary supplements such as iron and magnesium. Alterations to one's way of life can be an effective treatment for managing the symptoms of restless legs syndrome.

Talk to your medical provider if you have concerns that you could have restless legs syndrome. They can assist in the diagnosis of the problem and provide recommendations on treatment alternatives. Restless legs syndrome is not something that has to keep you from living your life normally if it is managed properly.

References

Contributors, W. E. (n.d.). Treatments for restless legs syndrome. WebMD. Retrieved October 19, 2022, from https://www.webmd.com/brain/restless-legs-syndrome/restless-leg-syndrome-treatment.

Dichtl, S., Haschka, D., Nairz, M., Seifert, M., Volani, C., Lutz, O., & Weiss, G. (2018). Dopamine promotes cellular iron accumulation and oxidative stress responses in macrophages. Biochemical Pharmacology, 148, 193–201. https://doi.org/10.1016/j.bcp.2017.12.001.

Eating with RLS. (n.d.). Retrieved October 19, 2022, from http://rlsfoundation.blogspot.com/2020/04/eating-with-rls.html.

Restless legs syndrome (Rls): Causes, symptoms, diagnosis. (n.d.). Cleveland Clinic. Retrieved October 19, 2022, from https://my.clevelandclinic.org/health/diseases/9497-restless-legs-syndrome.

Restless legs syndrome and related disorders information | mount sinai—New york. (n.d.). Mount Sinai Health System. Retrieved October 19, 2022, from https://www.mountsinai.org/health-library/report/restless-legs-syndrome-and-related-disorders.

Restless legs syndrome fact sheet | national institute of neurological disorders and stroke. (n.d.). Retrieved October 19, 2022, from https://www.ninds.nih.gov/restless-legs-syndrome-fact-sheet.

Seeman, M. V. (2020). Why are women prone to restless legs syndrome? International Journal of Environmental Research and Public Health, 17(1), 368. https://doi.org/10.3390/ijerph17010368.

Sullivan, G. (2018, March 5). 5 things to know about restless leg syndrome. Novant Health | Healthy Headlines. Retrieved October 19, 2022, from https://www.novanthealth.org/healthy-headlines/why-more-women-get-it-than-men.

What to eat if you have restless legs syndrome. (2019, August 30). Cleveland Clinic Health Essentials. https://health.clevelandclinic.org/what-to-eat-if-you-have-restless-legs-syndrome/.

Printed by BoD™in Norderstedt, Germany